Morna's Legacy Series

A McMillan Christmas

A Novella

Book 7.5

Bethany Claire

Editor: Dj Hendrickson
Cover Designed by Damonza

Available In eBook & Paperback

eBook ISBN: 978-0-9978610-0-6
Paperback ISBN: 978-0-9978610-1-3

http://www.bethanyclaire.com

For little Morgan

Welcome to the world, sweet girl.

Happy 1st Christmas

Chapter 1

On An Unknown Road In Scotland—December 18, 2016

I could barely see the road in front of me. Thick snowflakes the size of quarters fell so quickly that my windshield wipers couldn't keep up. Just as soon as one layer of snow was brushed away by the blades, another fresh coating took its place. To make matters worse, not only did the cheap tires on my standard rental feel less than secure on the icy Scottish roads, I was also helplessly lost.

The journey from the airport to my grandparent's new home in the Highlands was—according to them—supposed to take me three hours, tops. It was now two in the afternoon, and I was already on hour five of my drive.

The sudden vibration of the cell phone inside my coat pocket rattled me so much that I quickly pressed on the brakes and steered into the first pull-off I approached.

Pulling the phone out of my pocket, I hurried to answer before it sent my grandmother to voicemail.

"Hey, Gram. I know I'm late, but the weather is growing increasingly nasty as I continue north. In all honesty, it may be days before I get there. The visibility is very low and…" I trailed off as broken segments of my grandmother's voice interrupted my speech.

"Harper…Harper…I canna hear ye. Where are ye?"

Of course the reception was bad. As soon as I reached the edge of Edinburgh on my way out of the city, my signal dropped. Her phone call was the first sign that any reception had returned. It was part of the reason I was lost. Not only was the rental car place out of GPS navigation systems, the cell service was so nonexistent that I couldn't use the Maps app on my phone to get directions either.

"Gram, I'm going to call you back. I'm in a hole. Let me drive to the top of this hill, and I'll try to call you back."

I didn't wait for her answer. Ending the call, I shifted the car into gear and slowly made my way to a point of higher elevation ahead. It took longer than expected. I was forced to pull over four times for oncoming traffic. On the long, winding, one-lane road, I appeared to be the only one headed north. It only confirmed what I already knew—coming to Scotland was a mistake.

I suspected it the day I booked my ticket, knew it deep down when I boarded the plane, but watching all of northern Scotland fleeing south confirmed it completely. I was cold, frustrated, and near tears. I pulled over once again and returned my grandmother's call.

"Gram, is this any better? Can you hear me?"

"Aye, I can hear ye just fine. Do ye know where ye are?"

I didn't have the slightest clue. Five years had passed since my last visit to Scotland, and I'd only ever been in this part of the country with Kamden. At the time—fool that I was—I'd been too wrapped up in him to take much notice of what was going on around me.

"I really don't. I had to wait two hours at the rental car place, then all they had was a compact standard with no GPS. I've done my best to follow your instructions but, honest to God, I don't know how any of you get around. Nothing is clearly marked, and the weather is so bad I'm not sure I would be able to see the proper signage even if it was there."

Now thoroughly worked up, I struggled to take a deep breath and forced my tone to soften before I spoke once again.

"I'm sorry, Gram. I'm just ready to see you guys. Everything is fine. I'll get there eventually. It just might be midnight. Keep the lights on for me. Did you know the weather was supposed to do this?"

I should've checked it myself. I knew that Scotland had plenty of snow this time of year. Truthfully, too many memories had been playing through my head while packing for the weather to cross my mind.

Gram's long pause was answer enough. Eventually, when I said nothing, she relented.

"Aye, I knew there was a chance, but they hardly ever get it right. I was worried that if I told ye, ye wouldna come. All of this is my fault. I canna tell ye how sorry I am. Yer grandfather told me I should tell ye, but I just wanted to see ye

3

so badly. Now I've had ye fly all the way to Scotland and 'tis verra likely I willna be able to see ye anyway."

Gram's voice trembled, and my heart squeezed uncomfortably. I hurried to reassure her.

"Hey, it's okay. You can't take responsibility for the weather. Of course you'll get to see me—it just may be tomorrow instead of tonight. It will be okay. We are still days away from Christmas, and I'm staying through the New Year."

"Oh, my sweet girl, ye doona understand. I tried to call ye as soon as I saw that yer plane had landed to tell ye to get a hotel at the airport where ye could stay until ye got another flight home, but it never went through."

"A flight home? Why would I book a flight home?"

"Harper, we are completely snowed in. The road to our house is impassable, and I expect it to get far worse before it gets any better. Most of Scotland will be buried under snow come morning."

My grandmother continued to talk, but I no longer listened as her words replayed in my mind. Snowed in? Impassable? What was first an annoyance now presented itself as a real danger. At this time of year, it would be dark in only a handful of hours. If the vast empty land that lay behind me was any indication of what lay ahead, I doubted I would be able to find lodging anywhere close. If the road to my grandparent's house was impassable, then surely many other roads would be, as well.

"Harper, can ye hear me? Are ye listening?"

The worry in my grandmother's voice pulled me back into our conversation.

"Yes, I'm sorry. I'm listening. I'm just…I'm not sure that I'm going to be able to find anything before I reach roads that are too covered in snow, and I don't think I have enough gas to keep my car warm overnight."

The quick shuffle of the phone as it shifted hands told me just how frightened my grandmother must be for me. She'd never been one to handle any sort of crisis well, and my grandfather, God bless him, was always there to step in and save the day for her. If only all men were as wonderful as him.

I smiled as his deep, calm, and reassuring voice came over the phone.

"Ye and yer grandmother are cut of the same cloth. Both of ye lassies take a deep breath and calm down. Do neither of ye have any faith in me at all? I willna let ye freeze to death in the snow. If we can figure out just exactly where 'tis ye are, I'm certain I'll be able to think of a place ye can go. I know this country as well as I know the moles on my arm. If ye truly are good and lost, why I'll find myself a snowmobile and will go in search of ye."

I smiled at the confident humor in his voice. He must've been just as worried as Gram, but he hid it well. I would've given just about anything to see him zooming over the snow-laden countryside astride a snowmobile right then.

"Okay, thank you for that. I've no doubt that you would come and find me if it truly did come to that, but let's hope it

5

doesn't. I really have no idea where I am. How do you expect me to tell you?

"Firstly, bundle yerself up real nice and leave yer car running. Ye have winter hiking boots on, aye?"

"Yes."

"Brush the snow off the top of yer hood and climb atop so that ye may see better. Keep yer phone shielded in the hood of yer coat and tell me what ye see."

The prospect of stepping out into the freezing cold didn't thrill me, but I knew that in order to pinpoint my location, I would have to get a better grasp of my surroundings. I touched on the speakerphone and lay my phone on the dash so that I could ready myself for the wintery air that awaited me outside.

"All right, give me just a second. Can you hang on? Don't hang up. I'll let you know when I can see something."

"O'course, lass. I'll not be going anywhere until we've seen ye safely settled somewhere this night."

With my coat zipped, head covered, and gloves on, I placed the phone in my pocket, reached in the backseat for the window scraper, and stepped outside. I'd only been parked for ten minutes, and several inches of snow were already accumulated on top of the car. It took some effort to brush the bulk of it off. Once I managed, I climbed up onto the vehicle and reached back into my pocket for my phone.

"Okay, I'm here. Let's see…" I stalled while taking in the landscape around me. I sat parked at the top of a hill with a deep valley to my left and high terrain to my right. Rolling, snow-covered hills lay ahead. "All right. I just drove up a pretty steep climb so if I look behind me, it's a deep slope down. To my left is a large valley. There are no buildings or landmarks that I can see from that direction. Ahead is a winding road with three distinct dips and peaks. To the right, it's pretty much just straight mountainous terrain. I hope the snow doesn't cause any rocks to slip because I'm pretty certain I would be toast if any fell."

There was a brief period of silence. I could just imagine Gramps stroking his thick beard with his thumb and pointer finger as he tried to picture all that I told him.

Eventually when he spoke, his tone was filled with even more humor than before.

"Did ye say there are three distinct peaks in the road ahead?"

I lifted my hand to my brow to block some of the snow and strained to make certain.

"Yes."

"Turn yer head upward. Is there a rock at the top of the mountain that resembles a monkey?"

The snow made it difficult to see, but if I concentrated, I could make out the hint of such a shape. A memory tugged at the edge of my consciousness.

"Yes. The snow blurs it a bit but, yes, I do think I can see it."

"Lass, I know just where ye are. I believe ye know, as well."

The memory returned full force. I'd looked over this exact deep valley and stared up at the monkey rock once before.

I knew exactly what lay ahead—McMillan Castle...and the man who broke my heart.

Chapter 2

McMillan Castle

E veryone would be surprised to see him—Alfred, the tour guide; Henderson, the ticket salesman; Margaret, the cook; even the castle dog, Sileas, would find his timing surprising. It would be the first time in a decade he'd come home before the end of the castle's tourist season. If the weather predictions were correct, McMillan Castle was about to see the worst snowstorm of the past one hundred years, and he had no wish to make everyone that worked there spend Christmas trapped in the castle with him. Those with families should spend it with their loved ones. It wouldn't be his first Christmas spent alone.

As he pulled into the driveway of his old home, Kamden McMillan slowed his car to a stop, rolled down his window, and waited patiently for Henderson to recognize him as large, wet snowflakes floated into his car.

"Hello. Welcome to McMillan Castle. 'Tis a mighty cold day, but in my humble opinion, ye are about to embark on a discovery of the most magnificent castle in all of Scotland. Ye have come on a verra fine day, as well. Our head cook,

9

Margaret, has prepared her special Christmastime bread pudding. Ye willna want to miss it. After yer…"

Kamden watched as Henderson glanced up for the first time.

"Wha—what are ye doing here, Kamden? Why dinna ye tell me it was ye? I wouldna have kept blabbering on so."

He laughed and reached through the window to shake his old friend's hand. "I was enjoying yer sales pitch far too much. While I believe ye are over selling the experience, I appreciate yer efforts to bring people through the gates."

"Are ye staying through the holiday then?"

He nodded and shifted the car back into gear as Henderson opened the gates.

"Aye. What time does the next tour leave? I've got a mind to lead it myself."

"Oh, ye should. Everyone would love it. Ye've ten minutes to make yer way to the front doors. Best ye say hello to Margaret first, or she'll be right angry with ye."

"Aye, she would. Not a one of us wants that, do we? I shall enter through the back so that I can see her first. It's good to see ye. I'll visit with ye more at close today. I wish to meet with everyone in the sitting room this evening. Today shall be the last day of the season."

He drove away quickly so that Henderson couldn't question him. There were several cars already lined up behind him. If he got out of their way, perhaps they could make the tour he planned to lead.

The road from the gates to the side of the castle stretched the length of the large pond that lay in front of the castle. So many stories of magic were associated with the freezing cold waters of McMillan Castle—not that he believed in magic. If he did, he would certainly be calling upon it now, pleading with it to give him one more chance to make things right.

He shook his head to clear his mind as he neared the castle's side entrance. Melancholy thoughts would not help him give his castle guests the tour they deserved. Turning off the car's engine, Kamden hurried inside, stomping on the doorway rug to remove the snow from his boots. He could smell Margaret's baking and happily followed the smell.

When he entered the kitchen, Sileas, who lay happily at Margaret's feet hoping to catch some kitchen droppings, spotted him and let out his signature whine as he bounded toward him nearly knocking Margaret's feet right out from under her.

"Why, ye naughty dog. Do ye mean to make me break a hip? What are ye carrying on about?"

Kamden extended his arms wide as Margaret saw him. He braced himself for what was sure to be a rough impact as she ran toward him. He hugged her close as she reached him.

"I dinna expect to see ye for at least another week. Is the weather what has brought ye here?"

Of course Margaret would guess his reasons for coming early.

"Aye, but I mustna stay and visit just now. I've a mind to lead the last tour today. Do ye think Alfred will mind?"

11

Margaret kept a hand on his lower back as she ushered him from the kitchen.

"No, not at all. I expect he'll be verra pleased. He's come down with a bit of a cold. His voice has nearly left him completely. In truth, yer timing couldna be better."

"Good." He paused, the suggestion of his comment sinking in. "Not good that he's ill. Good that he will...eh, never mind. Ye understand what I mean. I canna wait to taste yer pudding. I'll see ye later."

Kamden bent to kiss her cheek and hurried to find Alfred before the castle's last Christmas tour.

On The Road To McMillan Castle

Is this outing truly necessary, Morna? I know ye feel that ye are rather invincible, and I suppose ye actually are, but 'twould do ye good to remember that I am not of the supernatural. If we crash on these icy roads, it could do me in."

Morna laughed as she sped across the snow-laden countryside, not reducing her speed a bit at her husband's words. After all the times she'd used her magic to bring people together through time travel, he should be accustomed to her shenanigans by now.

"Jerry, we've already discussed this. Of course 'tis necessary. Do ye really think I would be dragging either of us out in this weather if 'twas not? I have spent so much energy tending to the needs of my family that reside in the past that I've done a rather poor job of tending to relatives in the present. There is a lad verra much in need of my aid this evening."

"Does this lad know that he requires yer help?"

"Of course not. Do they ever? I hardly see how that matters at all, Jerry."

Jerry laughed. It pleased Morna to know that he didn't plan on being miserable for the entirety of their outing.

"Ye are right, love. It matters not. What of the lass— does she live in a time already past? Do ye mean to send him back?"

Time travel was her signature spell. While a form of it would be employed for her next pair of destined lovers, she had a new twist up her sleeve for this night.

"She lives verra much in the present—a modern lassie for a modern man. Aye, they will both travel backwards though in a different way than before. 'Tis a new spell. I verra much hope it works."

"Ye know it will work. They always do."

Morna could sense that Jerry was tense as she slowed her speed and turned into the driveway leading to the castle. The gate and ticket booth were closed and not a single car could be seen past the gate.

"I think we've arrived too late, Morna. It looks as if they've closed for the day. Mayhap longer than that if this weather keeps up."

13

She refrained from rolling her eyes at him. How had he not already guessed that she'd ensured they would arrive at precisely the time she intended?

"Jerry, I can see the castle is closed. 'Twill do little to keep us from entering. I wish to speak to the lad, and I'll hardly be able to do that if the castle is crawling with tourists."

"Aye, fine, but how do ye expect to explain yer sudden intrusion into the man's home?"

"Ye of little faith, Jerry. Why doona ye just wait and see? Follow my lead. I'll have us both back home in time for supper."

Chapter 3

"Has everyone cleared out? Ye dinna rush them, did ye?" Kamden directed his question to Alfred as all of the other castle workers began to fill the entryway. He knew the man felt terrible from the redness of his nose and the pasty pallor of his cheeks, but he'd specifically instructed that no tourist be ushered out of the castle until they were good and ready to leave. If he was going to have to close a full five days early, then he would allow the last tourists of the season as much time as they wanted to wander around inside.

"No rushing was required. I believe everyone can tell the weather is about to take a turn for the worst. I think they were all ready to seek shelter elsewhere."

"I doona doubt it." Kamden leaned to the left of the large doorway, glancing out the paned windows at a sea of white stretching beyond the front lawn of the castle all the way to the pond. The frosty waters of McMillan's pond were already beginning to freeze. By Christmas, it would be frozen through. "Where is Margaret?"

"I'm right here. Hold yer horses, ye impatient man. While everyone else's work ends when the last guest leaves, mine never ceases."

Kamden smiled and gratefully took the steaming mug of coffee Margaret extended in his direction.

"Aye, while what ye say is usually true, it is no longer the case. Not this winter. I have come home early to see this place shut down until well after the New Year. Weather reports predict record-breaking snowfall and ice. I willna have a one of ye out here putting yerself in danger. Nor will I have tourists wandering out here during such a mess. I simply want to meet with all of ye to tell ye to have the verra merriest of Christmases and to leave here at once. As always, I appreciate everything ye do for me here, but I can manage just fine for the time being without ye. Doona forget to pick up yer bonuses next to the doorway before ye leave. We will open back up in March."

Kamden knew the only protest would come from Margaret. Everyone else would be thrilled to spend a few more days with their loved ones before Christmas. What Margaret didn't know was that once he told her the surprise he had in store for her, she would be just as ready to abandon him as the rest.

"Ye surely canna mean me, as well? What will ye do for food? I willna leave ye here to starve. I believed I was to have five more days to prepare and freeze enough food to keep ye fed and well for the next month. I need that five days. I willna be leaving until my work is completed."

"Margaret, if ye insist on staying, ye may go to the kitchen and do what ye can for the next few hours. I'll see

16

everyone else off, settle myself into my chambers, and then I'll discuss yer early departure with ye in private. Make no mistake, I'll be seeing ye safely home before dusk."

He could see from the way her stance shrunk just an inch that she believed there was no point in arguing with him. Her surrender would be short lived. He had no doubt that by the time he went to see her in the kitchen, she would be ready to debate the matter with him once again. He waited until she turned and left the room to bid everyone else farewell.

"Ye are a fine man, Kamden. I would've sat at my post without complaint until the end of the season, but I did fear that the loss of my toes would be the price I would pay for my loyalty to ye. Thank ye for yer kindness."

Kamden knew that Henderson joked, but the man's words brought up a valid concern.

"Is there no heater in the ticket booth? Ye should have said something long before now."

"Aye, there is, but every time I open the window to greet the next guests, all the warm air disappears."

"We will come up with a better solution for ye before we open again. For now, go and ready yer home for all of the grandchildren I know must be headed yer way."

"Aye, they are. I canna wait to squeeze them."

The old man's build was broad and harsh, but his face and smile were friendly, and he never looked happier than when he spoke of his grandchildren.

17

The impending sadness of a Christmas spent all alone would be worth it to him if everyone he cared for could fill their holiday in the company of those they loved most.

Kamden opened his arms to hug Henderson. As the old man left, he said goodbye, one by one, to those that worked to keep his castle and home a wondrous delight for all its guests.

After he saw everyone save Margaret gone, he turned to grab his jacket, intent on gathering his belongings from his car. Instead, as he walked outside, he was met by an elderly couple making their way to the front door of the castle. Snow swirled around them, and they both looked like they were about to blow over from the force of the wind. Too shocked by their sudden appearance to say anything else, he hurried to offer them assistance.

"Let me help ye. 'Tis too cold for either of ye to be out in such weather."

The couple, both seemingly battered by the wind and snow, said nothing as he moved in between them and placed an arm around each to help them walk.

He glanced back at the castle gates as they moved together and was surprised to find them standing wide open. Henderson's car was already gone. It was unlike him to leave without making sure the gate was secured.

Once inside, he released his grip. The woman, after taking a moment to dust snow from her coat, spoke for the first time.

"Oh thank ye, lad. We had no idea the weather would turn so ghastly. No wonder we seem to be the only tourists here this day. Please tell me ye are still giving tours."

Kamden quietly took them both in for a moment. They'd appeared so frail to him as he watched them trudging through the snow up to the doors, but now as they stood brushing themselves off, they appeared anything but.

"Doona ye watch the news? This weather has been forecast for some time."

Kamden couldn't help but think that the old woman was a little too quick with her response to him.

"We doona have a television. Ye know how the forecast goes anyway. It seems they are only right half of the time."

While that was true, it still did little to explain their presence. Did they not notice the empty ticket booth even if the gate was open?

"Well, I canna disagree with ye. Excuse my rudeness, but ye must have passed the ticket booth on yer way here. Dinna ye notice that it was unmanned? I'm afraid that we've already closed for the winter season due to the weather. Allow me to escort ye safely back to yer car. I suggest ye hurry home and tuck in for the storm."

Neither of them moved at his suggestion. By their expressions, he didn't think they were surprised to hear that the castle was closed.

"I did see that the ticket booth was closed, but seeing as the gate was open and it is so verra cold outside, I simply assumed that ye had moved sales to inside the castle. Surely,

19

even if ye are closed, ye willna turn us away for we are here now and drove three hours to reach ye. My husband loves Christmas, and he has looked forward to seeing McMillan's Christmas decorations all year. Ye willna disappoint him, will ye?"

Kamden eyed the old man and saw nothing that resembled disappointment on his face. If anything, he looked rather amused at his wife's ramblings.

Regardless, the woman was right about one thing—they were already here. What would it really hurt for him to give one last tour of the season? If anything, Margaret would be thrilled to have two more people with whom to share her bread pudding.

"Right ye are. Why doona ye hang yer coats and follow me? I'll see that ye have the grandest of all tours."

Chapter 4

McMillan Castle

Normal group tours of the castle lasted exactly forty-five minutes. Alfred would show each group of visitors around the main common areas of the castle, bring them down to the castle kitchens, and then upstairs to see two of the castle's twelve bedrooms. The tour always ended in the great room. During warmer months, a tour of the castle gardens was also provided. Even during the Christmas season, when slightly more time was taken to explain the various decorations in each room, tours never lasted longer than an hour.

This tour, however, with its talkative and questioning couple, had already gone on for an hour and a half. Eager to see Margaret off before nightfall, Kamden eventually turned to address the elderly couple behind him, intent on informing them that their private tour had come to an end.

"And now, we've reached the end of our tour. All of the rooms past me are my own private chambers and are not open to guests. It would help ease my worry a great deal if ye would allow me to escort ye to yer vehicle so that ye may travel home before the weather grows worse."

The woman—who he now knew was named Morna— spoke as if he'd said nothing about ending the tour.

"Private chambers, ye say? Why, I've always wondered how a modern man would live in such an ancient castle. Surely ye have yer own rooms done up differently than the rest of the castle?"

He answered hesitantly. The woman seemed to be an expert at extending conversations.

"Aye...they have been altered significantly."

Kamden didn't miss the ornery lift of the old woman's smile. Dread filled him.

"Would ye mind ever so much if I looked inside? Ye giving us a tour made my husband's night, but this would truly make mine. If ye will only let me inside for a moment, I promise ye we will leave straight away."

Under most circumstances, he would have denied the woman's request. No guests were permitted inside this wing of the castle, but he knew there was really no harm in letting her look. He'd yet to unload his belongings from his car so he knew the room would be in pristine condition.

His arms were crossed, but he lifted a hand to point one finger in Morna's direction.

"Aye, fine. Ye may look but then ye must leave straight away. I willna have ye stuck out in this weather. And please doona take any photographs inside these rooms."

"O' course. Thank ye."

22

Morna smiled brightly at him as he reached to open the door to his living quarters. It stretched the length of the hallway. Rooms for any personal guests he might have lined the other side of the hall.

An idea occurred to him as he ushered them inside, and he hurried to follow through on it in order to ensure their quick departure from the castle.

"Why doona the two of ye look around in here all ye like? I trust ye not to touch or take anything. While ye look, I shall go and start yer car and bring it directly to the front door."

Morna's husband, Jerry, stepped toward him, whispering so that Morna couldn't hear.

"God bless ye man, for this and for putting up with my wife for these last hours. Ye are a saint among men. I would've turned us both away at the door."

Kamden smiled and gave the man a firm pat on the back. He'd known all along that the old man cared little about seeing the inside of his home.

"It was my pleasure. I'll meet the two of ye downstairs."

Kamden wasn't sure he should allow the couple to leave. The snow fell so thick and heavy that he doubted Margaret's ability to make it home, and she only lived a mile away. This couple had much further to go. Still, when he offered them a room, they refused it, and for a

23

reason he couldn't quite explain, when the old woman told him she could manage the trip home just fine, he believed her.

She hugged him tightly before they left. There was a grandmotherly grip to her hug that made him feel as if he'd known the eccentric woman all his life. Despite the poor timing and odd circumstances of their arrival, he found himself rather sad to see them go.

"What are ye doin' just standing out there? They passed through the gate long ago. Come inside and let me show ye what I've prepared for ye."

He turned toward Margaret's voice, brushing the snow off of his arms and shoulders as he walked.

"I'm sorry it took me so long. I dinna expect them to stay for hours. It would have been best if I'd denied their request for a tour."

"Oh, doona say that. 'Tis Christmastime. I'm sure yer kindness meant much to them. I've only managed to prepare a week's worth of meals for ye. I would really prefer it if ye let me stay here until Christmas Eve so that I may see ye better settled. I truly doona mind."

Kamden smiled. He couldn't wait to see Margaret's excitement at his news.

"Ye canna stay. Someone awaits ye at home."

He watched as Margaret's brows rose high on her forehead, but she showed no excitement as she eyed him suspiciously.

"Who? Doona tell me 'tis Emily and the babe. I may fall over from joy if it is."

Kamden took a step closer to her—just in case she actually did.

"I hope that ye doona fall, but I'll catch ye if ye do. Aye, 'tis Emily, the babe, and yer new son-in-law, too. I picked them up at the airport early this morning and saw them to yer home before I came here."

Margaret's arms came around him in an instant. He could feel her sobbing as he held on to her tightly. Her daughter lived in Australia with her new husband and baby, and Margaret had yet to meet either of them.

"Doona cry or ye shall make me cry, as well. I couldna verra well allow ye to miss the child's first Christmas, could I? Now, ye needn't show me a thing as I know verra well that ye have left detailed instructions on how I should heat everything. Gather yer things and let me see ye home."

Margaret pulled away just enough so that she could grasp both sides of his face. Tears filled her eyes as she looked up at him.

"I willna ever be able to thank ye enough for this kindness. Why doona ye join us for dinner? It breaks my heart to know ye plan to spend Christmas here all alone."

"No, ye need the time with yer family. I will be just fine here. It willna be my first Christmas alone. I've grown rather accustomed to it."

Margaret stepped away and frowned as she reached for her purse.

"No one should grow accustomed to such a thing. There is another out there for ye, I know it. 'Tis only that ye must open yerself up to the possibility of love again. Otherwise, it will never find ye."

He appreciated Margaret's optimism, but he knew that there was only one lass that would ever hold his heart, and he'd ruined any chance he had at holding hers long ago.

"Perhaps ye are right, though I doona think I'll open myself up to it this Christmas."

He turned without another word, leaving her to follow after him.

Chapter 5

On A Now-Known Road

"Gramps, I appreciate you helping me figure out where I am. Can you please hand the phone back to Grandma?"

I couldn't talk about this with him. Grandfather had always been far too fond of Kamden—even after the debacle of our breakup. He wouldn't understand my dismay over having to go back to the place where everything had fallen apart.

He said nothing, but I could hear the phone switch between their hands once again. Gram's tone was immediately empathetic.

"Harper, before ye say anything, I want ye to realize that I really doona think ye have any other choice for tonight. I know that does little to make it any easier. 'Tis only that I know ye, and I'm worried that ye will dig in yer heels and try to make do in the car overnight rather than go to the castle. Ye'll freeze if ye do that. 'Tis far too cold."

Most nights, she would've been right, but just a few minutes exposed to outside air had caused my joints to ache from the cold. I knew I had no choice.

"No, you don't need to worry about that, but yeah, it doesn't make it any easier. What am I supposed to say to him? I haven't seen him in five years. He's probably married by now. What if his wife is there with him? What if he has children there?"

The thought alone was enough to make my head spin and my stomach cramp uncomfortably. It would be hard enough to see him alone, but if someone else was there—a wife or a girlfriend—the liquor cabinet would need to be well-stocked to see me through this storm.

"Harper, he isn't married. Doona ye think I would've told ye if he'd gotten married?"

I didn't really know. It had been so long since I'd seen either of my grandparents and even when I spoke to them, they were both careful to never mention Kamden.

"Oh. Okay, well, good. Still, what do you think he will say? I know he will let me in, but I hardly think he wants to be snowed in with me for days on end."

"Sweetheart, if ye would stop speaking for more than three seconds, I could calm yer worries. Kamden willna be there. I saw Margaret a week ago, and she said that he wasn't due to arrive at the castle until Christmas Eve. With the weather the way it is now, I verra much suspect that no one will be at the castle."

A breath I didn't know I held released at my grandmother's words. The castle was empty. Not only would I have a beautiful, warm, safe place to stay for the night, but I

28

could enjoy it all without dealing with my ex-boyfriend. Sure, I would have to stare down plenty of ghosts of Christmas pasts in the castle, but I could manage the memories. I wasn't so sure that I could manage facing Kamden.

"Are you sure?"

"About what? I am fairly sure that Kamden willna be there, though I admit that I canna say for sure that no one will be at the castle. Though anyone that might be there will let ye inside. Only the Grinch himself wouldna let someone in on a night like this. Now, get off the phone with us and get yerself to the castle. Let me know when ye get there."

"I will. I'm sorry that I won't make it tonight. I'll get there as soon as I can."

"There is nothing for ye to be sorry for, Harper. We will see ye when the weather clears—whenever that may be."

As we bid each other farewell, I buckled my seatbelt and took off for McMillan Castle, hoping with each passing mile that the castle would be unattended and that Kamden hadn't moved the back door's spare key.

McMillan Castle

A hot bath would fix everything. His nose burned from exposure to the cold, and his legs ached from trudging through the snow. Nothing could have prepared him for such a long walk back. If his own car couldn't make it the mile back from Margaret's house, he was surely glad he'd insisted on bringing her home himself rather than letting her take her own car. Now, his car remained at Margaret's home, and Margaret's car was stowed safely inside the castle's old stables. Not that it mattered—no one would be going anywhere for days.

He very much hoped that the elderly couple from before made it home safely, for in this sort of Scottish weather, it wasn't safe for a single soul to be outdoors.

It took a long while for the bath water to run warm, but eventually steam began to rise. Kamden undressed quickly, placing the stopper in the bottom of the large copper, claw-foot tub as he slipped inside. He wished for every hot, scalding drop to touch his skin. He didn't remember ever being so cold before.

As the heat thawed him, thoughts of Harper swam through his mind. Baths always made him think of her. So did airplanes, scones, black and white films, and truthfully, just about everything else. He wondered what she was up to now— where she lived and whom she now shared her life with.

He wondered what she would think about the man he was today.

Sileas slept happily next to the tub. As the chill in his bones thawed, he closed his eyes, perfectly content to relax this way for the rest of the evening.

The spare key was gone, the old lock replaced with a numbered touchpad. I eyed the numbers nervously. The castle was surely hooked up to some sort of security system, not that I believed anyone would come and investigate a break-in during this weather. Even so, I didn't have any real desire to listen to sirens all night while I tried to sleep.

Kamden was a man of habit, of tradition. He never changed anything unless forced to do so. The rigid walls in every area of his life made him feel secure, and they are exactly what pushed me away.

I wondered what prompted him to change the lock. Had it been our break-up? Surely he hadn't worried I would ever break in. Although, as I looked at my current situation, I realized that perhaps that was no longer quite true.

My fingers hovered nervously over the keypad as I thought back on any important dates in Kamden's life. His birthday, his parents' anniversary, the year the castle was built—none of the combinations worked.

If the lock was like most, it would only allow me a few more tries before triggering the alarm system. On a whim, I typed in the only other date I could think of, the one date I was almost certain Kamden would no longer remember—the date of our first day of college—the day we met. Kamden and I both started college later than most people. There were just too many adventures we each indulged in before getting serious about our careers. It was our unique but shared early adulthoods that attracted us to

31

each other in the first place. To my everlasting surprise, the lock clicked open. Into the castle I stepped.

Sileas' sudden leap from the floor sent Kamden's eyes flying open, and water sloshed onto the floor as he sat up in response to the dog's high, eager whine at the closed bathroom door.

"What is it, boy? 'Tis only the wind. I'm sure ye've never heard such a sound in yer life. I know I haven't, and ye are much younger than me. Come here and sit down. Everything is fine."

Rather than calm the dog, his words only seemed to aggravate the great beast further. He whined even more loudly at the door. As if begging Kamden to let him out, he ran over to the tub and jumped up on its edge, pawing to get his attention.

"All right, all right, I'm coming." He stood, reaching for the warm towel hanging on its heating rack. He dried quickly and reached for a robe to cover himself as he opened the door to the bathroom.

Kamden expected the dog to calm once he realized no one was on the other side. Instead, Sileas took off like a rocket, out of the bedroom and into the hallway. He could hear the dog running and barking all the way downstairs. He knew the dog's sounds well. It was the same noise he made when Kamden came home only hours earlier.

Someone else was inside the castle. Someone the dog knew well.

I heard the dog coming only seconds after I stepped inside and closed the back door. I recognized his heavy footsteps and the distinct sound of his whine immediately—Sileas.

I couldn't help but smile as I hurried into the castle's main entry to greet him on the stairs. For the first two years of his life, Sileas and I had been the best of friends. It wasn't until he bounded up and into my open arms that I realized how much I'd missed the big, drooling beast.

I held and rubbed him, smiling and near tears at the joy I felt to see him once again. It took a long moment for realization to set in. No one would have left Sileas here alone in such weather. If Sileas was here, it meant someone else was as well.

I stood nervously and slowly lifted my eyes to the top of the staircase. Rather than the welcoming face of Margaret or Henderson, I was met by the tortured and shocked gaze of Kamden.

Suddenly, freezing to death in the car didn't seem all that unappealing.

Chapter 6

Many possibilities passed through Kamden's mind as he followed Sileas. Perhaps Margaret and her family lost heating or electricity in the storm and needed to seek shelter at the castle. God help them if they trudged through such weather with the baby. Perhaps Henderson realized he'd left the gate open after going home and came back to make certain it was closed. At least a dozen thoughts crossed his mind, but he never expected to round the corner and find his very own ghost of Christmas past staring up at him—Harper.

Five years without a word or a whisper of her, and now she stood on his stairwell.

"Ye cut yer hair."

If she wasn't standing before him, Kamden would've smacked his own forehead for saying something so stupid to her, but they were the only words he could muster. Just as it always had, the sight of her left him gobsmacked. Her hazel eyes, the shiny honey tint to her hair, the smattering of freckles across her nose, her beauty never ceased to make him smile. Her shape was different, firmer somehow, but overall she looked like the same beautiful woman. But she wasn't the same. Nothing was the same. He could see it in her eyes—the unfamiliar way she looked at him. They were now little more than strangers.

He couldn't imagine why she was here.

"Yes, I cut it some time ago. Look, I..." She hesitated and he saw her swallow. For a moment, he thought she might cry. It caused his chest to tighten in response.

"I never would have come if I'd known you were going to be here."

He didn't know how to speak to her. He feared whatever he said wouldn't relay how he truly felt—what he truly meant. "What are ye doing here then?"

Sileas balanced on his hind legs with his paws on the sides of Harper's hips, begging for her attention. Kamden looked on, waiting for Harper's answer. She continued to love on Sileas while she answered him.

"Trying not to freeze to death in this weather. You're pretty isolated out here. I didn't have many choices. I didn't expect you to be here. If anyone was here, I expected it to be Margaret or Henderson."

Of course she would come here if stranded. Anyone would. But what was she doing in Scotland? He didn't expect her to ever set foot in the country again. He remembered her swearing to as much the last time she left.

He took two steps down the staircase. Harper took two steps backwards.

"Aye, any other year, ye would have arrived to find them rather than me. I came home early when I heard reports of the storm. I dinna wish for anyone else to be stuck here because of it. They say it could last for days."

She nodded. An uncomfortable silence followed. They both realized what this meant. They would be alone here—together—for days on end. Facing their past was now inevitable.

I f not for the reassuring touch of Sileas' paw against me and the ability for me to hide my hands beneath the thickness of his coat, I knew Kamden would have seen me shaking. I hated it. How could he still have such an effect on me? Years had passed. Why was I not stronger? Why did the sight of him still seem to undo me so completely?

I could barely hear him over the sound of blood pumping in my ears. His voice sounded muffled and foggy. As he stepped toward me, I instinctively stepped back. I wasn't frightened of him, I just no longer knew how to interact with him. Everything about us standing across from each other felt foreign—as if I'd broken into a stranger's home to find the owner still there. It might have well been just that for the cold distance that lay between us.

One night in the castle with him would be hard enough, but only a fool would believe that the snow would be gone by morning. It would be days, possibly longer, before I would be able to leave here. It would take a miracle for me to make it to my grandparents' house by Christmas.

He stepped toward me once again. As if pulled by strings, I stepped back.

"I would never hurt ye, Harper."

I knew that. Yet I couldn't seem to control my body's need to distance itself from him in that moment. I planted my feet, grinding them into the staircase determined to not take another step as Kamden continued down the stairs to pass me. I could see the hurt in his eyes as he passed, but there was something else there as well, something that I couldn't quite put my finger on—something extraordinarily different about this man I'd once known so well.

It took his voice to bring me back to the present.

"I'm going to the kitchen. I've not yet looked at what she left, but I know Margaret cooked like a fiend this afternoon. Ye must be hungry, and ye look exhausted. Let's get ye something to eat."

I'd been both of those things earlier, but the shock of seeing Kamden shook me enough to make me forget my growling stomach and weary eyes. Adrenaline still coursed through me, making me shaky, nauseous, and wide awake.

Kamden was so calm and apparently unshaken by the sight of me. His reaction rattled me even more. While I hoped he would be gone, deep down I knew there was a possibility he would be at the castle. For him, this was his home. Nothing would have given him cause to believe I would come walking in the front doors in the middle of a snowstorm.

With Kamden gone, Sileas returned to all fours and headed for the kitchen. Reluctantly, I turned and followed him, speaking to my old friend as we went.

"Are you going to be the buffer between us, Sileas? I think we may need one. I fear that before this night is over, both of us will be in tears."

Sileas let out a knowing bark in response. Even he could foresee the inevitable trouble that would result from the two of us being locked up all alone here.

Chapter 7

In a flash of horror, it occurred to me as I entered the kitchen to see Kamden flinging contents of the freezer onto the center island—his robe hanging half open—that his state of dress for this time of evening was unusual for him. Had I interrupted something? Was he not alone here?

I'd not noticed his robe on the stairwell. But looking at him in his current state of dress, I felt foolish to have assumed he was alone. Gram's assurance that he wasn't married shouldn't have caused me such relief. Unmarried didn't mean alone. I should know that better than anyone. Kamden and I were inseparable for years, but we never married.

Just because I'd lived like a virtual monk for the past years didn't give me reason to believe that Kamden had done the same. Of course he hadn't. Men are terrible at being alone. And as much as I hated to admit it—his looks were enough to ensure that he never needed to spend a Christmas alone unless he wished it.

"Kamden, do you need me to leave here? Margaret's home isn't far. I'm sure she would let me stay with her. If I've interrupted something, I can go."

He froze with one hand on the freezer door and another buried deep inside it. He lifted his head and looked over his shoulder at me, his expression confused.

"What?"

"The way you're dressed—is someone else here?"

The lump that rose in my throat as I asked the question infuriated me. I hoped the fear hadn't come through in my voice. Kamden hadn't belonged to me for years. There was no reason for the thought of him with someone else to make me so emotional.

He glanced downward and smiled for the first time since my arrival.

"No. No one is here, though I doona expect ye will believe what I was doing when ye got here."

"Oh really? What were you doing?"

One corner of his mouth pulled up into an ornery grin that caused my stomach to flip over with a familiar sense of need. His smile always did me in.

"I was taking a bath."

I relaxed a little at his smile, and it seemed to me that some unseen wall crumbled between us. Not that it would make much difference—dozens more would have to be demolished for things to ever be normal between us again. Even if we were snowed in for a month, it wouldn't be enough time to accomplish that.

Still, it seemed that a pathway for communication was now open—one where I wouldn't have to worry about every little thing that I said to him. I hoped he felt the same way.

"No." I said the word on a shocked, disbelieving breath. I'd known cats who liked baths more than Kamden McMillan. "You hate baths."

I was a bonafide bath aficionado, but no matter how many times I tried to convince Kamden just how wonderful a bath could be, I'd never been able to get him to take one—even with me.

He flushed slightly but quickly turned away, burying his face in the freezer as he continued to rummage through its contents.

"They are not as terrible as I once thought them to be. Tonight, after trudging through the snow the mile from Margaret's house, one seemed especially appealing."

"Why did you walk all the way from Margaret's house?"

"I knew her car wouldna make the trip, so I parked it in the old stables and drove her down in my own. By the time I left, my own car dinna see fit to make the trip either. I was forced to walk back."

I shivered just thinking about it. It was a miracle he'd been able to manage it.

"Did that squelch any dreams you had of hiking Everest?"

He laughed and leaned back to close the freezer.

"Aye, 'tis funny that ye mention it. I was thinking just that about midway through the hike."

It didn't surprise me. Our thoughts usually followed along the same wavelength. Except when it came to matters of the heart.

41

Unless some miracle had occurred within the last five years, I knew that Kamden didn't have a clue what to do with any of the dishes he was so hurriedly placing on the center island. Even with Margaret's instructions, he would either burn the food or undercook it. With the initial surge of adrenaline subsiding, the growl of my stomach returned. I was far too hungry to let Kamden prepare the food.

"Why don't you let me pick something and start warming it up? You can go finish up your bath."

I moved from the doorway and made my way over to the island, not waiting for his answer as I began shuffling through the bags of frozen meals scattered on the counter.

"Aye, ye know better than to let me deal with the food. Thank ye."

I stilled as his hands gripped my arms from behind. Before I could turn or say a word, I felt his lips gently touch the back of my head.

"Harper, 'tis good to see ye."

He stepped away and left quickly, leaving me alone in the kitchen. I didn't breathe until I heard his footsteps ascending the stairs. When I finally exhaled, my breath shook with need.

I slumped over, leaning my elbows on the counter and covered my face with my hands.

I was in so much trouble.

Morna's Inn

"Jerry, come and see what I made wee Cooper for Christmas. 'Tis quite a bit larger than I intended, but I doona think it will be able to hold all the magic it needs to if I make it any smaller."

She could hear her husband's footsteps coming up the stairs, and she waited to say more until he entered. When his hands gently touched her shoulders from behind, she lifted it up for him to see.

"What do ye think? Will he like it?"

"It…'tis verra interesting. What is it meant to do?"

"Allow me to show ye."

She waved him back, knowing Jerry well enough to know he wouldn't wish to stand near her while she transported the gift backwards in time. It was an easy enough spell, one she used regularly for the letters she and the young boy sent back and forth to one another. While letters had always served the two of them just fine, Christmas was a time of magic. Why shouldn't she fill the young boy's life with just a little more of it?

"What exactly are ye showing me? Now that Cooper has the gift, how am I supposed to see what it does?"

Morna twisted and glared at her husband as she shook her head.

"Old age has made ye impatient and cranky. Give the child a moment to find it, will ye?"

Morna could sense the second Cooper picked up his gift, and she reached beneath her desk to retrieve her end of their new communication device—a small compact case, much like one she used to powder her nose. From the outside, Cooper's looked like little more than a pocket watch. Inside, it would connect him straight to her.

She popped the case open and smiled as Cooper's face appeared before her.

"Whoa, Morna, what is this? It's awesome."

"'Tis a new way for us to communicate. I made it small enough to put in yer pocket."

He frowned, and his little lip twisted uncomfortably.

"I don't have pockets."

"I bet if ye asked Isobel nicely, she could sew ye some. Doona ye think?"

"Yeah, that's a great idea. And she won't tell anybody what the pockets are for either."

Morna could see that Cooper sat on one of the castle's stairwells. What she meant to tell him, all of his family needed to hear.

"Are ye alone? If so, can ye go and gather everyone around? I need yer help this night."

Without saying another word, Cooper snapped the lid shut. She waited patiently for him to return. When he did, he was surrounded by all of McMillan Castle's residents—Mitsy, Baodan, Eoghanan and Grace, even Jane and Adwen stood in the background.

Grace spoke first, her tone gently admonishing.

"Morna, you spoil him. The letters are enough. You know that he'll never give you any peace now."

She ignored Grace. She would never cease to spoil Cooper whenever she could.

"As ye all know, I've a penchant for matchmaking. I canna help it. 'Tis my calling and it allows me to indulge in my intrusive and meddling nature. There is a descendent of yers, a man who has ended up far more alone than any in the room with ye will ever have to be. He misses his family, and he needs a second chance at love. I mean to show him the magic this night, and I wish for him to have access to it from now on. Ye all can give him part of the family he craves. I canna bring back what he lost, but I can connect him with what I can. Will ye welcome him?"

The response was no less than what she expected. It only took a few minutes for them to work out all of the details. She bid them all a Merry Christmas and a quick goodbye. When she turned to face her husband, he looked baffled and exhausted.

"How do ye ever dream up such schemes? Ye doona intend to only send the lad through one travel, but two? I fear ye have a better chance of putting him in a psych ward than mending his heart."

Morna hoped Jerry was wrong, but she couldn't deny that she was more nervous about this spell than most. Never before had one of her subjects endured two entirely different travels in such a short period of time. She just had to hope that the man and his lass were of sound mind and body. For if not, her Christmas would be spent repairing damage rather than enjoying festivities with her husband.

Chapter 8

Kamden changed and left his room quickly. It wasn't until he walked into the castle's great room and met the portraits of past McMillans face-to-face that shock set in. Thoughts moved slowly through his mind and his limbs grew suddenly heavy. Unable to continue his path toward the kitchen, he leaned against the room's back wall and slumped to the floor. He always sat with the room's portraits when he needed guidance. Now he needed their reassuring presence to reaffirm his sanity.

Had what he remembered really happened? Was Harper truly standing in his kitchen right now, warming a meal for the two of them after all this time? The chances of it were so slim that it seemed impossible. And yet, he knew that it was true.

He knew it if for no other reason than the fact that Sileas refused to follow him upstairs. If it were only the two of them in the house, Sileas would have been on his heels every step. But if Harper was here, Sileas would choose her company over his any day of the week. The castle dog adored her—always had. Although, he couldn't think of anyone that didn't adore Harper. In all the years he'd known her, he'd never heard anyone say a bad word about her.

She tried to hide her shaking hands from him, but he saw them before she slipped them into Sileas' coat. It was the first place his eyes had gone—his effort to measure if Harper's surprise at seeing him was genuine. Strong emotion of any kind always caused Harper's hands to shake. Nervousness, excitement, even anger would send her hands bouncing. They validated everything she told him—she never would have come if she'd known he was here.

At first glance, the briskness of Harper's tone and stiffness of her stature made her seem like a stranger, but once she joined him in the kitchen, he knew she was still the woman he knew and loved. He was glad for it. In his mind, nothing about her needed changing.

She was still the same bright, funny mind reader she'd always been. He loved how she could pick up on his thoughts before he said them. Just as he was about to suggest that she cook instead, she offered. It was always that way with her. She knew and understood him on an intuitive level that no one else in his life ever had.

In this dreary, dreadful storm, fate had blessed him with another chance. He was not the same stupid, frightened man of five years ago. He wouldn't let her slip through his fingers once again.

He would have to tread slowly with her. While Harper's strength still shone just as brightly through her hazel-colored eyes, there was hurt in them as well. Hurt he'd caused. Hurt that would take time to heal.

47

He hoped the storm would give them both enough time to return to one another.

Thirty minutes after Kamden went to change, I remained alone in the kitchen. While I'd never known him to take more than ten minutes to ready himself for anything, I understood why he took his time to join me. We both needed time to process. I was appreciative of the time alone.

After looking through the food that Margaret left, I chose an American favorite—meatloaf. The first year I dated Kamden, Margaret made it her mission to convince me of the merits of good Scottish cuisine. She never made anything other than traditional fare and quite stubbornly refused to let me cook. Despite her efforts, I never warmed to Scottish food.

By our second year, she started to believe that I was in it for the long haul and reluctantly began incorporating dishes that she knew were more suited to my tastes. They just so happened to be Kamden's tastes as well. For as much as he loved fried, fatty, dreadfully unhealthy foods, he should have been born in America. To everyone's annoyance, his body didn't seem to change one bit no matter how much junk he put in his mouth.

In the years since I left Kamden, much about my own diet had changed radically. While I'd never been overweight, I'd never been skin and bone either. My mother always called me "squeezable." Seeing as I didn't find anything wrong with the way I looked, the label never bothered me.

Once I left Scotland, heartbroken and angry, I needed an outlet—something to burn off all of my pent up energy. I found cycling and eliminated most of the crap from my diet. With time, my soft physique turned into a sculpted *I-bet-I-can-kick-your-ass* bod that helped to reinforce the *don't-come-near-me* vibes I worked so hard to put off. Pushing people away allowed me to control my own life, and it kept me safe from any other emotionally-stunted men that might wish to break my heart.

If someone had asked me only days before if I enjoyed my life of solitude, I would've said yes. Albeit, I have no doubt it would've sounded rather unconvincing. Now, I wasn't so sure about anything. I didn't know if it was just nostalgia or some long locked away part of my heart struggling to break free, but part of me longed to be the girl I used to be. I wanted to be the easygoing girl, the "squeezable" one who knew love and wasn't afraid of it. I wanted to be the girl that went to bed wrapped in the arms of another. Since I knew there was no chance of that girl returning to me tonight, I decided to at least allow myself the meatloaf.

Standing in his kitchen brought back the memories I knew were inevitable upon coming here. I doubted many people on earth were as complicated as Kamden McMillan. He was always kind, attentive, and funny with me and everyone else around him. In all our time together, I never saw him be unkind to any of his employees. Even as overwhelmed as he'd been during our first year together while he was trying to save this place, even with all of the pressure of being a full-time college student with a castle estate to run, he stayed level headed, thoughtful, and kind.

Kamden and I did everything together. We talked endlessly about everything. Everything, that is, except love. Kamden didn't speak about love in any context. I never heard the word come out of his mouth once. I understood why. The pain of growing up with a cold-hearted, closed-off toad made him weary of emotions. At least that's what he told himself and anyone that ever asked about it.

In truth though, Kamden showed love unlike anyone I'd ever known. He showed his love for his home by tending to the castle during some of its toughest times. He showed his love for his education by sticking with school despite all of his obligations here. His employees knew that he loved them by his countless acts of kindness toward them. If one of the castle workers needed their water heater replaced at their home, he would be the first person to see it fixed. When one of his tour guides found out she was expecting, he saw to it that she didn't lift anything heavier than five pounds until she went on leave. He was just that sort of guy.

I knew that he loved me, too. I never doubted it. He showed it in how he listened, expressed it in how he made love to me. I told myself that knowing he loved me was enough. I was careful to never tell him that I loved him either. I showed him in everything that I did and said, but if he wasn't willing to say the words, then neither was I. We continued like that for years. Until the day that he proposed.

On that day, our silent agreement suffered a swift, clean break. As much as I loved him, as much as I knew he loved me, in that moment, I needed to hear the words. I simply couldn't say yes without them.

In my joy at seeing him down on one knee, the words *I love you* slipped out of me easily—like I'd said them to him a thousand times. In my mind I had. I didn't even realize that I'd made a mistake until the smile fell from his face and his grip tightened on my hands. When he should've reciprocated my words—in that moment more than any other—he closed himself off to me completely—all while continuing to slide the ring onto my trembling finger.

My heart shattered in the middle of that awful silence that hung between us, and I realized that for me, knowing wasn't enough. I deserved more than he offered me in that moment.

Tears streaming down my face, I handed the ring back to him, walked over to where his car was parked and—leaving him stranded in the middle of a snowy field—I drove away. Some part of me always expected him to realize his mistake, sort through his issues, and come bring me back. He never did.

The memory no longer hurt the way it used to. For the first few years, each time I would play that scene over in my mind, I was filled with a mixture of heartbreak and rage that was so potent it would bring me to my knees. But with time, the feeling of loss decreased, and any anger that I felt for Kamden dissipated.

Kamden never meant to hurt me with his silence. If anything, I think my confession of love broke his heart, as well.

I'm not sure he realized what he felt for me was love. He believed himself safe with me. Once I said the words to him, his illusion of safety shattered. He'd fallen into the most powerful emotion any person can feel, all without his knowing it.

I stood peeling potatoes when the sound of Kamden's voice in the doorway caused my fingers to slip, sending the blade skimming across the end of one of my fingers.

I screamed and looked down to see blood saucing our side dish.

Chapter 9

K amden was beside me in an instant, ushering my hand into the flow of water he turned on as he reached for me.

"I'm not much in the mood for potatoes. Do ye mind if I throw them in the bin?"

Our eyes met as I glanced up at him, and we both burst into laughter.

"I should never be allowed around anything sharp. Yes, throw them in the trash."

He stepped away to clean up the mess on the counter while I washed my hand. When he returned, he rested one hand on my lower back while his other moved to guide my hand away from the running water.

"Ye need to bind this. Hold a towel against it. I will go and grab a bandage. What did ye choose?"

Once exposed to air, the sliced skin burned quite badly. I gripped it tightly and tried to ignore the fact that it still bled profusely.

"Uh, meatloaf. Is that all right?" My voice sounded strained and aggravated. I'd always been a big wimp when it came to pain.

With his hand still on my back, Kamden steered me out of the kitchen, up the stairs and to a giant leather couch in the middle of the great room. A fire burned next to it.

"Aye, I love it. Sit here. I'll return in a moment."

As soon as I relaxed into the sofa, Sileas jumped up and cuddled into me. I could still feel the touch of Kamden's hand on my back. Nervous, needy pinpricks raced up and down my spine. He was going to need to keep his hands off of me if I was going to manage to keep a level head over the course of the coming days.

Attraction didn't erase the past. Attraction didn't mean that Kamden could offer me all that he couldn't years ago. Attraction was little more than a physiological response to the memory of our shared intimacy. It was normal, natural, and completely ignorable.

By the time he returned with gauze and bandages, the bleeding had stopped. I attempted to pull the supplies from his hands, but he resisted as he crouched down in front of me close enough that his knees bumped up against the edge of my shoe.

"I'll do it. 'Twould not be verra easy for ye to manage on yer own."

Hesitantly, I extended my hand and braced for the warmth of his fingers as they touched my own. My hands began to shake on impact, and I could see a grin begin to spread from the corner of his mouth. Damn him. He thought my shaking was a sign of arousal. And it was, but I sure didn't want him knowing it.

"They're only shaking because it stings. You know how I am with pain."

"Aye, 'tis true I've not known anyone with as low a pain tolerance as yerself. Though, I was there when ye broke yer femur bone in two and yer hands dinna shake a bit then."

"You're an ass."

I didn't mean to be snippy with him—the words just slipped right out.

He laughed, and his next words only left me feeling more exposed. "I'm sorry. I doona mean to tease ye. 'Tis only that it pleases me to see that ye doona hate me completely."

He was taking a gamble with such logic. He knew that hate or anger could cause my hands to shake just as much as attraction, but I didn't see how arguing the point would help me. To continually deny it would only make him think I wanted him even more.

"I don't hate you, Kamden. I never did."

"Even when ye left?"

"Even then—especially not then."

My hand was now tidily wrapped, but he didn't release his grip.

"We need to talk, Harper—about all of it. I think we owe each other that much."

I agreed. I just dreaded it. In our current situation, a heart-to-heart was inevitable.

"We will, but only after I have food and several glasses of wine in my tummy."

I pulled my bandaged hand away from him, stood, and went in search of some wine.

He loved the way she looked when tipsy. Harper's bright, wide smile grew even warmer than usual, and the speckled flush of her cheeks only seemed to enhance the honey color in her hair. She was on her third glass of wine, but for the ease of her movements and the ever-growing thickness of her words, it might as well have been her fifth.

She ate more than he did at dinner, but he expected it was the only meal she had eaten all day. After so many hours in the car, she was probably dehydrated to boot. He would have to take the bottle and put it away soon. While it was tempting to sit back and let Harper get totally soused, he didn't wish for her to wake with a terrible headache come morning. More than that, he wanted her honesty, not drunken confessions of feelings she'd rather withhold from him. He wanted nothing from her that she wouldn't freely give.

He stopped after one glass. He wanted a clear head when speaking with her, to say everything he wanted and be of present enough mind to hear everything she had to say.

He saw his chance when Harper stood to examine the fireplace, wine glass still in hand. For the briefest of moments, her back was turned. He stood quickly and grabbed the bottle.

"I'll be back. I'm going to put the wine away. Then, may we talk?"

She waved him on without protest. When he returned, she held a small envelope and curiously extended it towards him.

"What is this?"

His first inclination was that one of the castle staff had picked up their Christmas bonus and then in the middle of saying goodbye to everyone, set it upon the mantle and left it, but as he reached for it, he could see that it was addressed to him. He read the words aloud.

"To McMillan Castle's master. I wish you the happiest of Christmases." His brows pinched in confusion. "Is this from you?"

"No."

She laughed as she answered him and drew the word out humorously. He thought she looked a little unsteady on her feet and gently guided her over to the couch.

"Well, let's find out who it's from then, shall we?"

The letter was closed with an old-fashioned wax seal. In the center of the wax were the initials M.C. It opened easily. As he joined Harper on the couch, he read the words silently to himself.

Dear Mr. McMillan,

Let me begin by giving you our most profound gratitude for the special tour you gave my husband and me this afternoon. It was a joy to see the love you have for this place. I personally know some of your ancestors very well, and it would please them immensely to know that their home has been so well taken care of for so many generations.

Now, onto the real reason for my letter. You, fine sir, are a practical man. I know this because I knew the man who raised you. I knew the man who raised him and so on and so on. I could go for so many years past it would make your head spin. McMillan men are sound of mind and immensely practical in all things. I beg you to let go of that practicality. For a world of miracles and magic awaits you this night.

So, are you ready? You must promise me to rid yourself of doubt and criticism before you continue. I'll give you a few minutes...Ready? Here we go.

As you know, my name is Morna. I'll not tell you what I am for I see no real need to go into it here. All that's important is that I care for you more than you know. I am so very sorry that your childhood was not filled with the love you deserved. As with most of us, our pasts shape us into the people that we are, but our pasts do not have to define our future.

Five years ago, you allowed that broken little boy to ruin the relationship with the woman you were meant for. You allowed your past to define your future. Broken-hearted little boys fear love. Grown men do not.

I know that my words may sound harsh, but I canna find it in myself to apologize for them. Sometimes those that love us need to shake the stupid right from us. Is that not what happened the night you dreamed of Baodan McMillan and his fair wife, Mitsy? That's right, lad, I know all about it for I was the one who put the dream in your mind to wake you up. And wake you up, it did. You learned your lesson and I am glad of it. Now, what you need is a second chance.

So now, enough with the lecturing—I'm ready to gift you a little Christmas magic.

I don't usually deal in the business of wish granting, but if you look to the earliest portrait in the grand hall, you will see the bonniest of your ancestors. His name is Cooper, and we are the dearest of friends. He often comes to visit me in this time. While he always says it is to see me, I know the truth–he really just misses his television and Disney movies.

Just last week, Cooper was over and we were watching the story of Aladdin and his big, blue genie. Have you seen this one? If not, I highly recommend it. I know I digress, but this genie gave me an idea. There always is a nice ring to things that come in threes, so I will follow the genie's pattern.

I'm gifting you three wishes: one for you, one for sweet Harper, and one that the two of you must make together. Your wishes must be made before going to sleep this evening. To make your wishes, do the following:

1. Upon the letter's completion, chunk this note straight in the fire. Harper need not see a word inside.

2. Say your wish aloud.

3. Have Harper do the same.

4. Repeat together.

5. Rest peacefully knowing that tomorrow will be a very different day for you both.

I've only one warning. Heed it well. For the love of all that is good in this world, wish for what you know you want the most. You've already made your wish a hundred times. Just wish for the same thing tonight. If you screw this up like you did your proposal five years earlier, I shall have to come and visit McMillan Castle once again, but this time it won't be the friendly, nosy, old lady version of me you saw this afternoon. It will be the angry, distant second-aunt (or whatever I am to you) version that is good and ready to slap, rather than shake, the stupid out of you this time.

That's right. We're related. Surprise!

Jerry says hello and to tell you that he had nothing to do with any of this.

Good luck and Happy Christmas.

Morna Conall

Chapter 10

Even with one more glass of wine in my system than was wise, I knew I'd never seen such a strange look on Kamden's face. The expression lay somewhere between fright and amusement. I couldn't figure out which one was the overwhelming emotion. Whatever the letter contained, he had no wish for me to see it. As soon as he finished reading it, he stood and chunked it in the fire.

"Was it that bad? Who is it from?"

"Ach, 'tis nothing. I closed the castle earlier today due to the weather. Just as I sent everyone away, an old woman and her husband showed up and asked if I would give them a tour. She was the strangest woman I ever met, though I dinna think her insane until this moment. I doona know why I burned it other than the letter said that I should."

He might as well have been speaking Mandarin for as little sense as all of that made, and I didn't think my slightly intoxicated state had anything to do with why I found it confusing.

"Why would she want you to burn the letter? And why is she insane?"

Kamden said nothing until he reseated himself. With Sileas still laying on the couch, I judged it safe to join him and sat on the other side of the dog.

"I doona quite know how to begin. I canna explain how she knew some of what she did."

I could see him working through all of it in his mind. His thick, beautiful brows were pulled in tightly, and he rubbed his forehead with the tips of his fingers—something he only did when he was tired.

"Why don't you start at the beginning? Talk through it with me."

It suited me just fine if we spent the evening discussing his mysterious letter and the crazy lady who left it for him. If he was distracted, perhaps he would forget to discuss anything related to us.

"Aye, fine. Oddly enough, the letter was just as much about ye as 'twas me."

"Great." When I heard the ridiculously sarcastic response to his statement escape my lips, I knew I was more into my cups than I thought. It was exactly what I was thinking, but I never intended to say it aloud. "Let me go get a big glass of water first."

He laughed and stood before I could move from the couch.

"I'll get it. I need one, as well."

It took less than a minute for him to return. He came back with two glasses of water and some aspirin for me. I smiled in thanks and quickly took the preventative painkillers.

"Okay, start at the beginning. How in the world could that woman know anything about me?"

As soon as Kamden twisted so that we faced one another on the couch, Sileas—the traitor—jumped up and went to lay by the fire. The space between us immediately seemed much too small, but I knew that moving would make my discomfort obvious.

"Well, she couldna know anything about ye. That is, unless she truly does have the powers she claims to have. Ye know as well as I the stories people tell about this and several other castles throughout the Highlands."

I expected I knew the stories far better than Kamden. While he grew up having the stories whispered to him by his grandfather's workers, I had intentionally learned as much about the tales as I could. In the end, resurrecting the rumors were what saved McMillan Castle after the death of Kamden's grandfather. People love believing there's the chance of magic lurking right around the corner. If they can go and explore a place where magic supposedly actually exists, they're all over it. Much to Kamden's chagrin, I'd been right that he should use the tales to his benefit.

Where the stories originated from, no one knew, but they all had to do with the castle's ability to send its residents back and forward through time. At least for several generations, that is. At some point, the ritual to ignite the time travel got muddled, and over time it changed so much that it no longer contained its power. By the time I started my research into the old stories, the old tale claimed that in order to travel backward, one had to gather a rock and spin three times while holding the rock above your head, all while standing outside on the castle's highest tower. Upon completing your spins, you had to chunk the rock into the castle's pond. This method didn't work. I knew. I tried it dozens of times with countless castle tours I helped lead during weekends and summers here with Kamden. It was the highlight of every tour.

You could see in the eyes of every tourist that some small part of them always hoped it would work. I'd always been one who enjoyed whimsy. Kamden hadn't. To even hear him suggest that the old woman might have whatever "power" he referred to was startling.

"Power…as in some sort of magic? You don't believe in anything like that."

He blushed slightly and something in my stomach flip-flopped in response to how attractive he looked when embarrassed.

"Ye are right. I never did. Though the night ye left, something happened that I've not told a soul. For if I couldna explain it to myself, I knew no one else would be able to help me sort through it either. This woman knew about it. I canna see how she could've known."

What intrigue—Kamden McMillan experiencing something that didn't fit into one of his tight, rational boxes of logic. I couldn't wait to hear more.

"What happened?"

He scooted closer—too close—so close that our knees touched. Then with absolutely no hesitation, he reached for my hands and gathered them into his own. My chest tightened and my breathing escalated. The only saving grace was that he held onto my hands so tightly they couldn't shake. At least there was that to save me from total humiliation.

"I'll tell ye, but it all relates back to ye. So first, I'll say what I've been trying to tell ye since I saw ye on the stairs a few hours ago. I know ye well enough to know that yer eagerness to speak of this letter is an avoidance tactic. Aye?"

"Maybe." I would give him no more than that.

He smiled and released his grip on one of my hands to reach up and brush a strand of hair away from my face. I drew in a shaky breath and closed my eyes, hoping every minute he would stop before I melted into him.

"Did ye know that until ye, Margaret was the only person in my life to tell me she loved me? I'm sure my parents did, but I doona remember them at all. And Margaret told everyone she loved them. I always rather thought she must not really know what love is either to use the word so freely. My grandfather raised me on his own. Not once did he ever say those words to me. The only time I ever heard him utter the word love was the day he told me just how dangerous such emotion was. 'We lose the things we love,' he said. 'Best not to love at all.'"

I never met Kamden's grandfather. He passed away just one week after we met, but I'd heard enough stories about the old man to form an unfavorable opinion of him. Still, to imagine a young boy growing up without ever having had that validation broke my heart completely. I couldn't imagine it.

"I'm so sorry, Kamden." The words fell short of what I felt, but I knew that my apology was not what he sought anyway.

"Ye doona need to be sorry, Harper. I am the one who is sorry, though 'tis no excuse for what I did to ye. I always knew better. My first love was a lass who lived just down the road. I was no more than fifteen. I loved her. I truly did. I knew it without doubt. If I remember correctly, I told her so only three months after our first date. My love for her dinna frighten me a bit. I remember thinking what a sad, lonely man Grandfather must be to have closed himself off so completely. I never bought into Grandfather's delusions about love. Through my whole life, I've allowed love to drive almost every decision I've ever made. It served me well until I met ye."

I didn't know what to say to that. If he meant to make me feel better about anything that had passed between us, it wasn't working.

"Kamden, are you trying to tell me that you couldn't return my feelings because you still love your first love more than you ever loved me? If so, that's totally fan-freaking-tastic, but there was no need for you to tell me that now. It just sort of rubs salt in the wound."

I tried to pull away from him, but he didn't allow it. Instead, his hands moved from mine up to my arms where he gripped me tightly.

"Harper, 'tis not what I'm saying to ye at all. I canna even remember that girl's last name. I told her I loved her on month three and by month five, I was with someone else whom I loved just as much. Do ye know the difference between the love

66

I felt for those that came before ye and the love I've felt for ye since the first moment I saw ye?"

I was at a disadvantage. I couldn't move away from his grip, and the need in his eyes was as telling of his feelings as my shaking hands were of mine. Any resolve I had to resist him was crumbling by the second.

"No."

His voice was hoarse and gritty, and there was a sense of desperation in it that caused my eyes to fill with tears.

"I've always known what love was. But before ye, the loss of love was worth the risk. I could fall in love, lose it, and survive. I knew from the start that wasn't the case with ye. I knew if I loved ye and lost ye, I wouldna survive the grief of it. But at the same time, I couldna keep myself away from ye. I thought that if I kept ye at a distance and never admitted it aloud, I could protect myself from my grandfather's miserable fate. I was a fool, Harper. Denying love does nothing to prevent pain. It only makes it worse, for 'tis the loving that makes pain bearable."

He could sense that I no longer wished to pull away. His hands moved from my arms to my face where he brushed away my tears before leaning in to place his lips on mine.

Chapter 11

He knew he should stop himself. There was still so much he needed to say to her, so much he needed to explain, but God, she felt good pressed against him. Her desperation seemed to match his own. She opened herself to him, easily accepting the swift dip of his tongue as he explored her mouth with an insatiable hunger.

He lost himself when she moaned beneath him. As he slid his hand over her breast, all thoughts of conversation left him. It was only when she stilled and pushed him away that any sensible thought returned.

"I'm sorry, Harper. I—" She interrupted him before he could say more.

"You don't need to apologize for anything. I think...I just don't think this is very wise."

It was entirely wise. Kamden had no plans of ever kissing anyone but her for the rest of his life. Though he knew he couldn't say that to her—not yet. She was already too flighty around him. Instead, he nodded in agreement, lifted himself from on top of her, and pulled himself together as much as he could.

"Ye are right." He could only vaguely recall the last words he said to her before the kiss. Luckily for him, her memory seemed to return more quickly.

"What made you realize all of that, Kamden? You referred to something that happened the night I left, but you never said what it was."

The dream—at least that's what he thought it must be. Though it was so unlike any dream he'd ever had that he found it difficult to believe that was truly what it was.

"Do ye remember my fondness of these portraits?"

Harper twisted to look at the row of faces behind them. The movement exposed her neck to him, and by the light of the fire, he could see how flushed her creamy skin still was. It caused his groin to ache dreadfully.

"Yes. You told me once that you would talk to them all the time growing up. That if you had a problem, you would come to them and somehow just talking things through in their presence helped you to sort things out."

He smiled. She never forgot anything.

"Aye, and it always did. The night ye left, however, 'twas not enough to speak to them. I needed to hear back. I was alone here. I sent everyone away shortly after ye left, spent the evening raging in front of these portraits, damning them for not being more help, damning my ancestors for dying and leaving me here to sort all of this out on my own. I drank too much and fell asleep by the fire. In my dreams, I was amongst them." Kamden paused and pointed to the earliest portrait so Harper

69

would follow his meaning. "Not with them in reality. It was more like seeing the movie of their lives playing out in my mind.

"I saw Baodan McMillan's heartbreak at the death of his wife. I witnessed the betrayal of his brother, and I understood his pain. But then I watched as he moved out of that darkness, toward love once again.

"Whether any of what I saw actually happened to these people, I suppose I'll never know. What I do know is that seeing my own kin suffer such heart-wrenching loss only to open his heart up to the possibility of pain once again showed me that not all McMillans are destined to end up like my grandfather. Love was a choice for this man. A choice he made while already knowing true loss.

"Distancing myself from ye at the same moment I asked for yer hand did nothing to protect me from pain. All it did was betray the trust ye placed in me by offering me yer heart. I loved ye, Harper. I was simply too much a coward to say it.

"I will be a coward no more. I loved ye then, and I love ye now. And these words now will not be the last time ye hear them cross my lips. I shall tell ye every day until ye forgive me—every day until ye believe them and know in yer heart that I am not the same man I was then."

Chapter 12

I believed him. I believed he meant every word he said. That didn't mean it was enough to change anything. He could tell me he loved me every day until this blasted snowstorm came to an end and then call and tell me he loved me every day after, and I doubted it would ever shift what was now broken inside my heart.

What Kamden didn't realize was that his confession of love didn't change anything for me. I always knew that he loved me. I knew the day I left—I was just no longer willing to be with someone who refused to say it aloud.

Five years of stifled heartbreak and anger erupted from me in one quick motion. Before I knew it, the little wine that remained in my glass splashed onto Kamden's face as I stood from the couch and glared down at him.

"You're an idiot."

Kamden's big green and infuriatingly beautiful eyes nearly bulged right out of his head as he tried to wipe away the wine with his fingers.

"Of all the ways I imagined that going, I dinna ever imagine that."

"Case in point, Kamden." My voice dripped with sarcasm.

He stood, his eyes shocked and angry as we glared at one another.

"Just what exactly did ye find so offensive? Forgive me, but I canna see it."

"I know that you 'canna' see it." I hated myself for poking fun at his accent. It insinuated that I didn't like it, and we both knew that wasn't true. But I was too wound up to reign myself in now. Calm had no chance of finding me until everything was out in the open. "That's exactly the problem. The day I left...was that the first disagreement you ever had with anybody in your life?"

I didn't wait for him to answer. I didn't really care.

"I walked away from you that day because I'm not foolish enough to agree to marry someone that won't tell me they love me, but I didn't realize this relationship was over until four weeks passed without a word from you.

"I stayed in Scotland for four weeks waiting for you to work through your shit. All while genuinely believing that once you did, you would come and find me. I left word with Margaret about where I would be, and I waited for you. You never came. Even after I went back to the States, I kept expecting you to show up."

I was screaming at him, sobbing in between shaky breaths. I didn't realize until that moment just how much pain I had carried with me all these years.

Kamden looked horrified and suddenly much older than he was. I couldn't tell if he wanted to gather me up in his arms, or turn and run into the blowing snow and hope for the best.

When he said nothing, I continued. Now that I was speaking about all of it, it felt like opening an artery, and I couldn't seem to stop the flow of words.

"Why didn't you come and find me? The second you woke up from that dream and you knew your mistake, why didn't you come? Do you think I wanted to take that stupid job in Boston? I didn't. I wanted to be here with you. And now...how am I supposed to feel after everything you've just told me? It would've been easier if some grand revelation hadn't come to you. Then I could go on believing that the reason you never came for me was because you were still just as broken as you were then.

"Now, though, I know that you weren't broken. You just didn't love me as much as you thought. For apparently, it never even crossed your mind to ask me to come back to you."

I couldn't deal with the conversation a moment more. Whatever he could say in response to me, I knew it wouldn't make me feel any better.

Turning away from him, I gently clicked to call Sileas to my side, and I walked from the room.

"Where are ye going?"

Kamden's voice followed after me. I could hear his steps approaching, but I didn't look back, and I didn't say a word until I reached the room across from his. I would spend the night here, without my bags. I couldn't bear to say another word to him until there were walls between us.

Once inside, I slumped back against the door, waiting for the questions I knew were bound to come from the other side. I could feel him out there sitting just opposite of me. He waited. When he finally spoke, his voice sounded just as tortured as my own.

"Harper, I did look for you. I looked everywhere."

Margaret would never lie to him. She was the closest thing he'd ever had to a mother.

"I wish that I could believe you."

"I've never lied to ye."

"I don't know what you've done. Not anymore. I'm tired. I just want to go to sleep. Please leave me alone."

"Aye, fine. I wish that we could go back in time—to our last days together. I would do things so differently."

I didn't answer him as I stood and moved to the bed. Instead, I whispered my response so that only I could hear.

"Oh Kamden, I wish we could, too."

Betrayal surged through him as he walked away from Harper's door. Witnessing her pain was heart-wrenching, but to hear her say that she'd wanted him to come for her? Nothing could have hurt him more.

He went to Margaret the moment he woke from his strange dream so many years ago because he knew that Harper

74

wouldn't have left without telling someone where she was going, but Margaret told him that Harper didn't want to be found, that she never wanted to see him again. When he sought out her grandparents, they had moved. Margaret told him that they'd gone to somewhere in the States to be with Harper. He'd had no reason to distrust her.

Despite Margaret's misgivings, he still searched, but Harper never told him about a job offer in Boston. Without anything to go on, his search got him nowhere. Years he'd lived thinking she hated him, thinking she never wanted to see him again. All the while, every day he left her out in the world alone he was breaking her heart all over again.

Margaret's betrayal felt as if his only tie to any sort of family had just been severed completely. It baffled him.

He crawled into bed like an animal, a sense of desperation clinging to him so tightly that no thought of Morna's instructions crossed his mind as he drifted off into an angry sleep.

His last conscious thought was one of family—a wish that those who helped him once before would give him guidance once again.

Chapter 13

I stood in the back corner of the castle's kitchen watching as Margaret chopped away at a heaping pile of vegetables. I called to her, but my voice sounded distant. She didn't respond. She didn't seem to see me either.

I lifted a knee to move but couldn't step forward. Baffled, I tried again but to no avail. Something invisible prevented me from moving. I called to her again, but my voice only reverberated off whatever unseen wall stood between Margaret and myself. Panic blossomed inside me. Just as I opened my mouth to scream, Henderson entered the kitchen. I paused—Sileas was at his side, and the dog was visibly younger than he truly was—he was little more than a pup.

The sight of Sileas relaxed me. I was dreaming. Of course I was. It made sense. The invisible wall, the sound of my own voice coming out strained and distant—it was like one of those nightmares where you open your mouth to scream and nothing comes out. Only, this dream was lucid—I knew that I was dreaming. My thoughts in no way seemed sleepy or distorted.

I remembered reading about such experiences in college—lucid dreams often allowed the person to manipulate his or her own dreams. Now that I was aware I was sleeping, there was no reason why I should still be blocked by the invisible barrier. I lifted my knee and leaned forward only to be thrown backwards against the counter once again.

I still couldn't move. Maybe one had to be practiced at lucid dreaming to alter the state of their dreams. Whatever the case, at least I knew that this state of frozen suspension would end.

Henderson's voice filled the room, and knowing there was no longer any harm in being unable to move, I stopped trying to fight against the barrier in front of me and listened in.

"What did ye just tell him, Margaret? I've never seen Kamden so upset."

"I told him precisely what he needed to hear. Someday he will thank me for it."

I watched on as Henderson spread his hands flat against the island and leaned forward to look down at Margaret's small stature.

"And what did he need to hear? I hardly think that is for ye to decide."

Margaret shifted uncomfortably on her feet, and a sense of knowing spread through my limbs. Sileas' age should've clued me in sooner. This dream was the time right after I left.

"I told him that Harper dinna wish to see him again and that she dinna tell me where she was going."

"Is it true?"

Margaret's silence caused Henderson's face to flush bright red.

"Do ye know what ye've done, Margaret? Do ye think lying to the lad will stop him? He'll just go to her grandparent's house. Then he will know ye lied. He will never trust ye again after that."

When she answered him, Margaret's tone sounded pleased. For the first time, I found myself glad for the barrier. Without it, I feared I would've lunged for her neck.

"Do ye think I'm such a fool? I thought of that. Harper's grandparents are away for the holiday. They went to the States to see her parents. When they return, they'll be returning to their new home up north. They've just sold their place in Edinburgh."

Henderson's question reflected my own.

"Why would ye do such a thing? They love one another. What place is it of yers to keep them apart?"

"I've been the only one to watch out for that boy for his entire life. He never had a mother. Someone needs to act in his best interest."

"He'll be thirty next week, Margaret."

"That matters not. Harper knew what she was getting herself into when she started dating him. He treated her like royalty. If that wasn't enough for her, then good riddance—he deserves better than to be humiliated and left out in the cold."

"Neither of us know what happened between the two of them last night. Ye know the lad as well as I do. He's a good man, I'll not say otherwise, but he can also be a damned fool. If I were a betting man, I'd wager that the lassie had good reason to leave. Regardless, none of this is our business."

If I ever saw Henderson again, I would kiss him for his defense of me.

Margaret set her knife on the counter and crossed her arms in defiance.

"Ye are right. None of this is any of yer business at all. What I say to Kamden and what I doona say is of my concern, not yers. Will ye tell him?"

"Aye, I will. I'll not let yer petty meddling interfere in their lives."

Margaret's voice lifted three octaves to a screeching tone that caused Sileas to whine.

"Petty? Meddling? I care for him, Henderson. His heart is broken. If that is what Harper did to him, I doona ever want her around him again."

"I thought ye liked Harper."

"I thought I did, too, though it seems I dinna know her. He could've done nothing to deserve such treatment."

Henderson shook his head in disgust and turned to leave the room, but Margaret's voice stopped him before he took his first step.

"Wait. I thought I would give ye the opportunity to agree to keep this secret, but ye have not done so. If ye tell Kamden any of this, I shall tell Kamden yer little secret. Do ye really think he would keep ye on here if he knew ye'd taken half of last month's ticket sales for yerself?"

When Henderson faced her, the redness in his cheeks was gone, replaced by a sickly whiteness that made me fear he would drop to the floor.

"How do ye know about that?"

She laughed. I found myself disliking her more with every word.

"How could I not know? I make the deposits each week when I go to get groceries. I see how many guests come through these doors. The money hasna added up for some time. I doona know what caused ye to do this, but I know the sort of man ye are. I know that if ye would take from Kamden and this castle, ye must be in dire need of it. I doona want to do this, but if ye tell Kamden what I've done, I shall tell him straight away."

"Fine. I thought I knew ye Margaret, but ye can rot in hell for all ye have done. I'm sure I shall join ye for being yer accomplice."

As Henderson left the room, the barrier in front of me gave way and my mind began to spin.

The dream was over.

He stood before his ancestors but apart from them, an onlooker on the past and nothing more. He could see and hear them but not interact as he wished. He wanted more than to see their lives play out in front of him. He wanted to speak to them, to know that he was not so alone and that some of his family was still available to him.

This scene was different—earlier than the events he witnessed before. On second glance, he could see that this dream wasn't in the past at all. Or at least, it wasn't as far back as his dreams took him last time. There was a car behind him and three people stood in front of him.

He knew them all. Morna stood on the banks of the pond with her husband a few paces behind her. Next to them stood a red-haired woman with an ornery glint in her eye.

Mitsy—the lass he watched Baodan McMillan fall in love with during his dream so many years ago. But what was she doing in the present with Morna and Jerry? Did that mean the tales about his ancestors were true? That Baodan had married a woman from the future? How had he not picked up on that as he watched their story play out before him last time?

Dozens of questions raced through his mind. Yet he knew he was unlikely to find answers to any of them.

Sarcasm dripped from Mitsy's voice as she spoke to Morna and Jerry.

"Oh, right. How stupid of me. Are you joining me, or am I jumping on the crazy train alone?"

Kamden had no idea what exactly she referred to, but his eyes moved to the smooth rock in Mitsy's hand. The stories always referred to the use of a rock. His pulse quickened as he watched the scene play out before him.

Mitsy turned away from the old couple defiantly.

"I don't need to practice."

She reared back, flicked her wrist, and let the rock loose.

Kamden watched as it bounced off the water. Once. Twice. Mitsy turned to speak.

"See, three times…"

Before she could finish her sentence, Kamden watched as the lass disappeared.

Everything went quiet around him. As he stood still in the distance, Morna and Jerry got in their car and drove away.

Kamden knew all of this could be a dream and nothing more, but if it wasn't, he now knew how to use the magic that eluded his ancestors for so long.

The surroundings around him whirled together. Kamden knew his dream was approaching its end.

Chapter 14

McMillan Castle—December 19, 2011

I didn't wake once the dream ended. For several more hours, I enjoyed a dreamless sleep, content to be warm in the bed with Sileas by my side. I woke to a surprisingly bright beam of light hitting me in the face. Yawning, I stretched out my legs and raised my arms above my head and out to the sides in the hopes some movement might pull me from the deep sleep. When my right arm hit something solid, I screeched and flew out of the bed so quickly that my ass hit the floor with a big thud.

Scampering to my feet, I looked at the bed. Kamden lay sound asleep. My first impulse was to scream at him, to whack him with a pillow and shoo him from my room, but then my brain caught up with my eyes, and I realized that Kamden wasn't in my room. I was in his.

Wine was the devil's poisoned apple. If three glasses of wine got me so wasted that I unconsciously stumbled into Kamden's room in the middle of the night, I would never touch the stuff again.

The sunlight continued to ping the back of my head. Twisting on impulse, I turned to look in its direction. When I saw outside the window, I reached out a hand to steady myself against the windowsill.

As expected, snow covered the ground outside, but rather unexpectedly, the dangerous accumulations of snow, the piles and piles of it, were gone. The sun was out, and any sign of the storm that sent me to the castle for shelter was gone.

I gripped my head as I fought the overwhelming confusion that gummed up all other thoughts in my mind. How could the snow have melted so quickly? By the time I fell asleep, I was entirely sober. How then had I ended up in Kamden's bed without memory of it? If I was going to sleep with him again, I sure as hell wanted to be able to remember doing so.

The sound of footsteps in the hall sent me into a panic. It was only when Sileas barked at the approaching sound that I looked at him for the first time since waking. Just as in my dream the night before, Sileas was young. Remnants of puppy still clung to his little face, and his bark didn't have the same deep tone that it had now.

None of it made sense. Perhaps I was still sleeping? Only in this dream I wasn't frozen in place. On the small chance that it was true, I hurried back to the bed, crawled inside, and pulled the covers all the way over my face and shut my eyes as tightly as I could manage.

Nothing happened.

Instead, the footsteps of whomever approached Kamden's room now stopped right outside the door, and someone was calling for me to answer it.

"If the two of ye are still abed, I can let Sileas outside. The last day of tours starts in an hour. Ye know how Sileas likes to greet the guests."

With Kamden still snoring beside me, I crawled back out of the bed and very hesitantly walked over to the door where I cracked it open. The second I did so, Sileas was off the bed and running down the hall.

"Whitney? Is that you?"

I'd not seen the young housekeeper since leaving Kamden, but she didn't look a day older for it. She looked back at me with an expression of confusion that matched how I felt.

"Aye, o'course 'tis me. Are ye and Kamden still leading today's tour together? Alfred said that ye were, and when I told him that the two of ye were still asleep, he almost came up here to wake ye himself. I told him 'twas best if I did so."

"Oh. Well, thank you." Terror dripped down my spine, but I couldn't see how letting Whitney in on my own insanity would help matters. With as much coolness as my shaky voice could manage, I responded matter-of-factly.

"Yes, we will lead it."

Then, I closed the door in her face and stood there with my hand still gripping the bedroom doorknob until I could no longer hear her footsteps retreating down the hallway. Once she was gone, I locked the door and ran over to Kamden where I gripped onto both of his shoulders and shook him as roughly as I could.

That's when I really knew I'd entered the twilight zone. My arms could scarcely lift him even a few inches off the bed. All of my strength was gone. I glanced down at my arms, my legs, and to my horror, my slightly pudgy mid-section.

"Kamden. Kamden. Wake the hell up. Something…something is going on here and I am freaking out."

He stirred, but my nudging did nothing to wake him. I stomped toward the bathroom, reached for the rinsing glass next to the sink, filled it, and then walked back over to the bed. Without hesitation, I threw the water in his face. His eyes flew open as he gasped and sputtered and sat up in the bed.

"Wha…why do ye keep doing that to me?"

I'd forgotten all about the wine incident from the night before.

"Just wake up. Something is happening to me."

The panic in my voice must've concerned him for he was up and out of the bed in an instant, reaching for my arms as he tried to calm me.

"What is it? What's wrong?"

I pulled away and pointed toward the window.

"Go and look out the window."

I was certain my hands had never shaken so violently in my life. It took me crossing my arms to still them as I watched Kamden move across the room. He looked out the window for a long moment. When he finally turned towards me, unbridled confusion etched his face.

"How long did we sleep?"

"I don't know, but that's not the only thing, Kamden. I woke up this morning in your bed. I have no recollection of coming in here last night."

His brows raised as he sat on the bed.

"Ye dinna come in here last night. I would remember that."

I threw my hands up in exasperation.

"I would remember it, too, but I'm telling you, when I woke up, I was lying next to you in that bed."

Kamden's fingers moved to his forehead, just as they'd done while reading his letter the night before.

The letter. Some far off question begged me to acknowledge it, but I was far too shaken up to think about it just now.

"That's not even close to being all, Kamden. Look at me."

His hand dropped from his face, and he looked up.

"What about ye?"

I approached him while motioning to my untoned arms. Then I dramatically pointed toward my gut.

"I did not go to sleep looking like this."

"I like the way ye look. Always have."

"That is not the point. You know that I didn't look like this when I went to bed."

For the first time since waking, Kamden smiled. Really smiled. A big, goofy grin that made me want to slap him. I screamed at him in exasperation.

"What is the matter with you? Do you think this is funny?"

"Aye."

I did hit him then, lunging toward the bed as I whacked his arm in frustration.

"It's not funny. Something seriously weird is going on here."

"Aye."

I felt sick. Dizzy sick. So sick that I feared I would vomit right on top of him if some sort of sanity didn't find its way into my psyche soon.

"I swear if you say 'aye' one more time, I'm going to throw myself out that window. What is going on?"

Casually, as if it were the most normal thing in the world, Kamden said, "Morna's letter was true, lass. Our wishes worked. We went back in time."

Chapter 15

I listened quietly for a long time as Kamden explained to me the contents of the letter he received the night before. I knew that while he'd attempted to explain everything last night, it all derailed after our kiss and my reaction to his confession. Every bit of it was hard to believe, but I couldn't very well argue with the reality of it as I was living it. By some strange miracle or curse—I guess only time would tell which one it was—Morna's magical letter sent us back to our last Christmas together.

"There is only one thing I doona understand. Ye made yer wish whether ye knew it or not. Ye said that ye wished ye could believe me. I made my wish, unknowingly as well, before I went to bed. I wished for my family to help me once again, but we never made a wish together. How then, did we end up here?"

I replayed the events from the night before over in my mind and I knew right away.

"We did make a wish together. You just didn't hear me. I didn't really want you to. When you told me that you wished we could go back to our last days together, I whispered that I wished so, too."

"Ah."

That pleased him. I could see it in the way he grinned at me. An unusual feeling of closeness filled the space between us. I expect it was the fact that whatever this strange turn of events might mean, we were going through it all together.

"Did your wish come true?"

He crossed his arms.

"I'm not sure. In the midst of sleep, I thought aye, but now I see I'm missing one verra special component of the magic."

"Meaning?"

"Much like the dream I had five years ago, I watched events of a past time happen before me. Though, this time, I watched the real time travel ritual take place. We've been doing it wrong for a verra long time."

"I know."

I laughed, panic subsiding with each moment we spent talking through the crazy that was this day. As unbelievable as every bit of it was, I no longer found it worthy of window-jumping panic.

"How's it done, then?"

"First, we must have a magic rock spelled by the same Morna who left us the letter. Then, 'tis really rather simple. There's no need for climbing up the tower or spinning in circles. Ye simply skip the stone across the water. On the third bounce, ye disappear."

Any normal day, it would've seemed absurd. Today—not so much.

"Of course. That's much more sensible than the way we always did it with the tourists. Problem is, you don't have a magic rock."

He stood and disrobed in front of me without a second thought.

It should've shocked me to see him standing there in his underwear, but knowing the time we were now in somehow made it seem okay. In this time, we were together. In this time, I saw him naked all the time.

"Precisely. Alas, I doona have a magic rock." He stepped away and moved into the bathroom where he reached into the shower to turn on the spray. "Would ye like to join me?"

I swallowed hard as he removed the rest of his clothing and stepped inside. I shouldn't look, but he just made it too easy.

"Uh no, better not." I had to raise my voice so he could hear over the water.

"Suit yerself. What about ye? Did yer wish come true? Is there any chance that ye believe I looked for ye now?"

I started to answer him, but he interrupted me as he opened the shower door and leaned outside to speak.

"I canna hear ye. The glass is all steamed up now anyway. At least come and sit in here and tell me."

"Fine." I walked backwards into the bathroom and stood still just to the right of the shower door. Just thinking about my dream enraged me.

"Yes, I believe you. I had a similar dream to yours. It was the weirdest experience of my life. You need to fire Margaret."

He hesitated and then said rather sadly, "So, 'tis true then? I had hoped there was another explanation."

I knew it must pain him to hear of Margaret's betrayal. He loved her dearly.

"Yes. I'm sorry, Kamden."

"What did ye see?"

I told him what I could, omitting the parts about Henderson's transgressions. Margaret had been right about one thing—he would never steal unless something extreme was going on in his life. If Kamden had remained ignorant of it for over five years, I saw no need to deliver one more piece of hurtful news to him now.

When I finished, Kamden turned off the water. Before I could move away from him, he stepped out of the shower and wrapped his arms around me. I gasped and tried to break free, but he clung too tightly.

"Kamden!" I shrieked at him. "You're wet. You're soaking my clothes right through."

He laughed into my ear. My entire body came alive as his warm breath traveled down my spine. His naked body pressed flat against my back, and I had no desire to move away.

"These are yer night clothes. Ye must shower and change if we are to lead today's tour. If we are correct and we really are back five years in the past, 'tis the last tour of the year. We gave the group quite a show last time. Let's not disappoint them this time around, aye? Then once everyone is gone, we will sit down and try to figure all this out."

Years of misunderstanding and hurt still lay between us, but two very important things were already healed inside my own heart. First, Kamden loved me and he'd said it. Two, it had never been his choice to stay away from me.

It certainly wasn't everything, but it was something. Standing there with him, his arms wrapped around me, my nightgown becoming more see-through by the second, I didn't have the strength to fight him anymore.

It was a new day. A new time, even. Perhaps, this was our second chance to get things right.

Twisting, I faced him and wrapped my arms around his neck.

"Is it too late to take you up on the shower offer? We have to be downstairs in half an hour. I might be able to get ready more quickly if you help."

He groaned as I kissed him. Much to my surprise, he quickly pulled away, though there was a smile in his voice as he left the bathroom.

"I'm afraid 'tis, lass. Ye know how I hate to leave our guests waiting. Doona worry, I'll make it up to ye later."

I took a deep breath, turned the water to cool, and breathlessly jumped beneath its spray.

I couldn't wait to get this tour over with.

Chapter 16

Approximately twenty-five minutes later, Kamden and I were both dressed and ready to head downstairs for the tour. I remembered this day well. I could even remember the faces of most of those we would soon see downstairs for the castle tour.

Most castles in Scotland closed for the winter season. As I knew firsthand, travel wasn't especially easy in the winter, and it wasn't the peak of tourist season anyway. McMillan Castle benefited greatly from most other castles being closed. While tourism was definitely down in the winter, there were always some visitors keen to visit the country regardless of the weather or time of year. By decorating McMillan Castle with gorgeous Christmas décor and throwing in some holiday activities with the tour, the castle quickly became a must-see destination if visiting Scotland in the winter.

"Are ye ready for this? Do ye remember enough to help lead it? If not, I can manage on my own. Ye could experience it as a guest."

I knew he meant the offer as a kindness, but I couldn't help but feel a little insulted. I loved this castle as much as he did. I didn't imagine that I would ever be able to forget its history.

"You just wait. You won't be able to tell that I missed a single tour. I remember everything."

I left the bedroom first. I wanted to gather up the guest roster from Henderson before the tour started. It was always nice to have the guests' names in front of me. More often than not, I could guess the name that belonged to each person just by looking. It was a special talent that annoyed Kamden to no end. It was always my favorite thing about the tour.

I was keenly aware of how strange it was that all of this felt normal to me. Walking down the castle's staircases and corridors, gazing up at the Christmas décor as I made my way to the front entrance, it felt as if the last five years never happened at all. For now, I didn't even really care.

It was nice to be back in an easier time before everything fell apart. Even if I woke to find all of this was a dream, even if it all went away tomorrow, I could see no harm in enjoying it while it lasted.

All thoughts of joy went away the moment I stepped into the main entryway. I expected to see Henderson coming through the front door with the list of names. Instead, Margaret stood in his place holding the clipboard and pen.

"You." I hurled the word at her like an insult as I stomped over in her direction.

She couldn't have looked more confused. Assuming I joked, she mimicked me, pointing a finger in my direction and with a shocked tone she said, "You."

I didn't smile or laugh. Instead, I ripped the clipboard from her grip and stood there angrily.

I wanted to scream at her, to tell her she was fired and toss her stuff right out the front door, but I knew it wasn't my place to do so. Margaret was not my employee.

Kamden was only a few steps behind me. While I expected him to—at the very least—treat Margaret with the same icy coolness I had, he instead gathered her up in a big hug and kissed her cheek before pulling away.

"Good morning, Margaret. Is it not a fine day? What are ye doing in here? I expected ye to be in the kitchen."

She smiled at him, and my blood boiled. I knew what traitorous thoughts lay beneath that smug smile of hers.

"Aye, 'tis lovely. Though it seems the world has gone topsy turvy today."

She had no idea.

Kamden looked around as if looking for something amiss.

"What do ye mean?"

"Alfred is in the kitchen watching the scones for me, and I've taken over Henderson's position."

"Where is Henderson?"

"He is helping one of the guests change a flat tire."

"Ah. Do ye think he can manage it on his own?"

Margaret nodded and nudged her head toward the door.

"O'course he can. The two of ye have a tour to lead. The group is waiting just outside."

I couldn't believe how polite Kamden was being to her. It should've upset him even more than me.

"Margaret, would ye mind welcoming everyone inside while I speak to Harper a moment? We just want to practice our entrance."

Margaret agreed, and before I could say a word, Kamden dragged me into a dark hallway on the other side of the entrance hall.

"What were ye about to do to Margaret before I came in here?"

I crossed my arms and didn't blink as I answered him.

"Fire her sorry ass."

He laughed but quickly gained his composure as he lowered his voice to plead with me.

"Harper, doona ye remember where we are? As of now, Margaret has done nothing to deserve yer hatred of her. We canna verra well punish her for something she hasn't done."

"But she will do it. We already know that she will."

He placed his palms on either side of my face and kissed me gently before pulling away to look down into my eyes.

"No, she willna do it. For things are not going to happen the same way they did last time. Besides, I doona believe there was malice in Margaret's choice."

I wanted to believe him. While I was willing to enjoy things as they came, neither of us could know for sure if we had any power to change how things occurred between us last time.

"You don't know that."

He didn't seem shaken by my lack of faith.

97

"Aye, I do know. Things are already different. Five years ago, 'twas not Margaret that greeted us at the door, and none of our guests punctured a tire on the way up here. If those changes can happen, so can many others."

Perhaps he was right.

"Fine. I will say nothing to Margaret, but I mean nothing. I don't want to see or speak to her and that's exactly what I'm going to do."

He kissed the tip of my nose and took my hand as we went to welcome the tour.

"As long as ye doona insult her or pull her head off, I doona care."

When we stepped into the entryway, a dozen tourists stood waiting. I was good with people, but Kamden came alive in front of strangers. His warm welcome had them all smiling and laughing before he even introduced himself.

We played off one another well. Kamden stuck to the history, and I filled in the yawn-worthy stuff with all the tales of whimsy. It was a good group—not too big, not too small—and all the faces were exactly the same as five years before. With a quick glimpse at the roster, I remembered each of them.

Kamden always saved the great room for last. It was by far the most breathtaking room in the castle. From its large fireplace and portraits to the massive Christmas tree at its end— it was a guest favorite every time.

It took only seconds for me to spot it when we entered the final room on our tour—the velvet sack sitting right above the fireplace where Morna's letter had been the night before. I didn't falter in my story as I walked over to the mantle and pointed to the portrait of Kamden's father to direct their gaze in another direction as I reached to grab it.

It was heavy, and I knew right away what it was. Sidestepping over to Kamden, I gently placed the bag in his hands. He looked at me and mouthed his question, "What is it?"

Shrugging, I walked away to finish my speech, but when I looked back at him from across the room, I knew I was right.

A big, smooth rock lay in the palm of his hand.

Chapter 17

The moment he concluded the tour, Kamden moved to Harper's side.

"Meet me in my study. I'll show the guests to the kitchen and leave them with Margaret. I wanna speak to ye about this."

When she nodded and took the rock from his hand, Kamden turned to see the group downstairs. It took some time to corral them. Many wanted pictures with him by the tree. Others wanted him to sign their souvenir books. It was unusual for the owner of such a great castle to interact with guests. As much as he wanted to speak with Harper, he wouldn't deny them the unique experience of having some time with him.

"If ye are all ready, I'd like to take ye to the castle's kitchen. It is the most updated part of the castle—a necessity to keep our dedicated cook, Margaret, happy. She's prepared some special treats just for ye. Then, our usual tour guide, Alfred, has arranged sleigh rides around the pond for all of ye. If ye still wish to take pictures in the great room, doona worry. Once ye've finished all other activities, ye are free to wander around the castle on yer own, just as long as ye are out of the castle by five this evening. At that time, Harper and I will be leaving for a verra special trip. Christmas Eve will be our fifth year together. I plan to propose."

He smiled at the anticipated "oohs" and "awws" from his guests. Knowing they would have time to wander on their own seemed to do the trick, and they gathered around him without delay as he led them downstairs.

Margaret waited for them at the bottom, a basket of scones in her arms, the kitchen bar lined with mugs of hot chocolate.

"Do ye and Harper wish to join in? I've prepared a mug for each of ye."

He stood by Margaret's side while the group filed into the kitchen. Once all were inside, he turned to speak to her.

"Thank ye, but no. We need to finish packing for our trip. I'll see ye before we leave."

She waved him on, and he rushed toward the study.

He couldn't wait to cancel their trip.

His family awaited both of them in the past.

I never doubted that a magic rock would show up somewhere. Not after my wish was granted in my dream and our mutual wish was granted when we woke up in the past. The rock's appearance seemed inevitable.

Five years ago, Kamden and I left for a trip to the swankiest and most secluded resort in the Highlands. I suspected that this time around, Kamden had other plans in mind. He always longed for family. If this rock truly had the power to bring them to him, he would take it.

Kamden's study lay on the ground floor of the castle at the very end of the primary corridor of the staircase. It ensured total privacy when he wished to spend hours going over the books or, as was usually the case, just wanted a moment to breathe.

I roamed around the room taking in all the memories of years past. Photos of our college years together were scattered around the bookshelves that lined each wall. While each one made me smile, they were also a reminder of all that crumbled between us the day I left. I hoped Kamden was right. I hoped things could be different this time.

"I like that one of ye."

I didn't know he entered until I heard his voice behind me. I leaned into him as his arms came around me. He bent to rest his chin on my shoulder as we gazed at the photo of me in my cap and gown.

"You can't be serious. You can tell I've been crying—my face is all red and puffy."

"I never saw anyone less eager to graduate college. Ye loved every minute of it."

I had. College brought me to Scotland—the only place in my life where I ever felt truly at home.

I pulled away and went to pick up the rock sitting on the desk. It could've been my imagination, but it even felt magical.

"So...we're not going north, are we?"

He smiled and shook his head.

"I called and cancelled our reservation as soon as I left the guests in the kitchen. I wish to take ye on another trip instead."

"Do you think it will work?"

I hoped that it would. His disappointment would be overwhelming if it didn't.

"Aye. I do. I canna see why the witch would leave it for us if it wouldna. I doona wish for the staff to know about it. We shall have to resort to trickery."

"Trickery, huh?"

He had everything planned. He was quick that way. He could come up with plans on the fly with ease.

"Aye. They will wish to see us off. The staff is staying on until Christmas Eve even though our last tour is now done. I say we leave in the car as planned, then take the back road to Margaret's house and park the car in her old shed. 'Tis unused, I know, and I doona believe she's opened it in a decade."

Nothing sounded less appealing.

"If we do that, we will have to walk a mile back here. It will be freezing."

He nodded apologetically but didn't back down.

"Aye, 'twill. But if we park the car on the side of the road, someone will see it. I doona wish for them to be concerned about our wellbeing. We will wait until dark to skip the rock. That way, we will be able to leave unseen."

103

At least we wouldn't be hiking in the middle of the snowstorm of 2016. As long as we bundled up, we would be fine. Uncomfortable, but technically fine.

"Okay. How long until we leave in the car?"

Kamden glanced down at his watch.

"Two hours."

"Great. Are we packing?"

He thought about it for a long moment before answering.

"I doona think so. What do we have that would belong in the past? I say we just go with the flow, lass."

Laughing, I agreed. It was all rather exciting, really. Wherever the rock sent us, I supposed it would be an adventure. The past years of my life had been much too void of risk. I would make up for it now.

"All right. I've got something I need to take care of. Do you think Henderson is back in the booth?"

He eyed me suspiciously.

"Aye, I expect he is closing everything up. Why?"

"Good." I pulled him toward me and kissed him until both of us were breathless. "I'll meet you in our room in an hour. Maybe you can make up for abandoning me in the shower, then?"

That distracted him enough to stop his questions.

I took off in search of Henderson.

Chapter 18

I heard Henderson's chair shift from inside the old ticket booth the moment I knocked on the door, but it took me calling out for him to answer.

"Henderson, it's me, Harper. Let me in. I'm freezing out here."

There was another slow shuffling sound and then, finally, he opened the door.

"Harper, what are ye doing out here? Ye should've told me it was ye from the first. Almost every day we have some guest try to come in after I've closed the booth. I'm accustomed to ignoring the knock on my door."

"I just wanted to come and see how you were doing. Mind if I sit?"

He must've been suspicious of my answer right away, but he said nothing to indicate he was. Instead, he smiled and ushered me to one of the two chairs that sat inside the tiny space. In peak months, Kamden hired seasonal help to man the other booth window.

"How did the tour go? It seemed a fine group."

"It went great. Maybe the best one ever."

The old man smiled, his crooked, yellowed teeth just barely peeking out in the middle of his silvery beard.

"I'm pleased to hear it."

An awkward silence settled between us. I loved Henderson, but I'd never really had much conversation with him outside of normal niceties. It was odd for him, too. His eyes roamed around the interior of the booth uncomfortably.

Eventually, I decided it was best to be frank with him. He wouldn't appreciate anything else.

"Can I ask you a question?"

"O'course, ye can."

"Henderson…are you in some sort of trouble?"

Whatever he expected me to ask, it hadn't been that. His mouth visibly opened and closed at least three times before he answered.

"How did ye know?"

I couldn't very well tell him the truth. Instead, I tried to come up with the most believable lie. The only thing I could think of was to tell him that I'd been making the deposits. There was a chance he would know that wasn't true, but it was the best thing I could think of in that moment.

"Margaret's been so busy lately doing her usual end-of-year assessment of the kitchen and preparing food and goods to hold Kamden over for the next few months that I volunteered a few weeks ago to take the deposits into town and pick up the groceries for her. Did you know that I majored in accounting in college? It doesn't take long for me to see when numbers are off."

Even that was a lie—I held a degree in Shakespearean literature, but I didn't know how Henderson would ever be able to call my bluff on that.

He crumbled the minute I asked him the question. The pain and guilt on his face was so evident that I moved to gather him up against me as he started to cry. My heart broke for him. Before I knew it, I sat there and cried right along with him. I said nothing. There was no need for me to. In a moment, he would gather himself and explain. Whatever the reason, I could feel nothing but sorrow for whatever position he was in.

When he did lift his head, he apologized profusely.

"I'll pay every bit of it back, I swear to ye. Did Kamden send ye because he was too angry to speak with me himself? I doona need my last paycheck. I shall gather my things and not ever come back here again."

I reached for his hands and tried to reassure him with my grip.

"Hey, it's okay. Kamden doesn't know anything about it. He's not angry, and I'm not either. We know you, Henderson. I just want to know what's going on so I can help."

"Nothing could justify the trust I've betrayed. My reason matters not."

I continued to insist.

"It does to me."

For a long while, I thought he wouldn't tell me. He sat thinking for the longest time, then he pointed out the booth window toward the building on the other side of the trees.

"Last month, Kamden asked me to take out the old snowmobile and get it running again. He thought there would be enough snow to use it this year. So, I spent two weeks working on the machine, and I finally got it running. Problem was, I dinna know how to drive it. I turned it on, but instead of backing it out of the barn, I plowed it through the front."

My hands flew to my face in shock.

"Did it hurt you?"

He shook his head and the tops of his cheeks uncovered by beard turned bright red.

"No, though the barn is in right bad shape. I couldna tell Kamden, for he would've fired me and rightly so. I would've fired me, too. I doona make enough to pay for its repairs on my own. I've pulled aside a little this month to cover the cost. Though, I never would've done so if we had not had the busy summer that we did. I swear it to ye."

I would've burst out laughing if not for the distraught look on Henderson's face. I truly expected him to confess to some sort of gambling addiction, not for him to tell me that he was so prideful that he would rather steal than admit to a mistake. If it could even be called stealing—the money was going right back into the castle.

"So, you're not even using the money for yourself?"

He looked appalled by my question.

"O'course not. What sort of a man do ye think I am?"

"A stupid, prideful one. Kamden would never fire you for something like that, and you know it. You were simply too embarrassed to tell him."

"Aye, I am. Please doona tell him, Harper. I'll pay the castle back. 'Twill only take me some time."

"You won't do any such thing." I pulled my checkbook out and looked him straight on. "How much have you taken?"

"I willna allow ye to pay for this, Harper."

His arguing was pointless. I held the upper hand and he knew it.

"Yes you will. How much?"

He looked down shamefully.

"Three thousand pounds."

Swallowing, I tried to hide my astonishment as I wrote him a check.

"Cash this, put the money back in next week's deposit and never say a word to anyone about this."

Reluctantly, he took the check from my hands.

"Why would ye do this for me?"

"I'm doing it because you're a good man, even if you are stupid. You came to my defense once even if you don't realize it, and I want to do the same for you now. Just promise me one thing."

"Anything."

"If there is ever a time when Margaret asks you to keep a secret for her, promise me that you won't do it. Promise me you'll tell Kamden."

His wiry brows pulled together.

"What do ye mean?"

"It doesn't matter. Just promise."

"Aye. I promise. Thank ye, lass."

109

I stood and wrapped my arms around him in a big hug.

"You're welcome. Merry Christmas, Henderson."

I breathed easily on my walk back to the castle. At least now we had a safety net. While things were pleasant now, Kamden and I were both opinionated, fiery people. It was still very possible everything would be shot to hell by the time the week was over.

If so, and everything ended up just how it had the time before, at least Kamden would be able to find his way back to me.

Whether Margaret wished him to or not.

Chapter 19

An hour away from her was absolute torture after such a teasing statement. What did Harper expect him to do for that long? He started by getting two empty suitcases from his closet and filling them with random clothes, shoes, and blankets before placing them by the door. They would need to be heavy enough to not raise suspicion.

Once that was done, Kamden took to pacing the room with Sileas by his side. He couldn't wait for her to return. How many times had he dreamed of making love to her over the last five years? Countless times. But each one only left him wanting her more. She couldn't possibly understand the hunger he had for her now.

She would find out soon enough.

I knew what awaited me on the other side of Kamden's bedroom door. I could sense him from all the way out in the hallway. The intensity of it halted me in my tracks. I wanted to weep for how badly I wanted to feel him inside me, but that need didn't mean I wasn't freaking terrified.

So much time had passed. What if things were different between us? Even though kissing him was enough to turn me into mush, what if our real sexual chemistry was gone? Or what if I was just so rusty that he found himself questioning if his memories of our past were accurate? Either outcome horrified me and left me paralyzed outside the door.

I must've done something to make Kamden aware of my presence, for just as I was about to turn around and flee, the door opened and he pulled me inside.

"What are ye doing standing out in the hallway?"

"Deciding whether or not to run and make an excuse for it later."

He tilted his head to the side in question.

"Run? Why would ye do that?"

Kamden's green eyes were as lusty as I'd ever seen them. His gaze traveled down my neck as I spoke and locked on the dip between my breasts just as my breathing escalated in response.

"I…" His hands slipped beneath my shirt and slowly slid upward as he bent to kiss my neck. I could hardly breathe. "Do you want me to be honest?"

He answered as he trailed his lips along my collarbone.

"Always."

"Kamden, I'm terrified."

He stopped his act of delicious torture and lifted his head to look at me seriously.

"Terrified of the stone or of me?"

Our plan for that evening had nothing to do with my fear.

"I'm not worried about tonight, and it's not that I'm scared of you, exactly. I'm afraid of this. It...it's been so long, Kamden. What if I'm really bad at it now? What if it isn't good?"

He smiled and gently lifted my hand so that he could kiss the inside of my palm. The sweetness warmed me through.

"Lass, I'll not have ye worried about a thing whilst in my bed. Memories of yer skill in matters such as this are seared into my memory forever."

I groaned and retreated until my back hit the wall.

"I know. That's what I'm afraid of."

"Harper." He stepped toward me, his expression desperate and needy. "I've never wanted anything as bad as I want ye right now. 'Twas always our love for each other—even unspoken as it was—that allowed for such wondrous lovemaking between us. That hasn't gone away. If anything, it has grown stronger with every night I spent apart from ye."

His hands were on me again, slowly tugging and lifting my shirt until my arms lifted to assist him. On impulse, I reached to remove his. In moments, all our clothes were scattered on the floor. He lifted me with ease, and my legs wound around him as he walked me over to the bed.

"'Tis like riding a bike. Let me show ye how little ye have to be afraid of."

113

I lost myself in the sensation of loving him. As he entered me, I cried out his name. We moved together in a familiar rhythm that only comes with the most seasoned lovers.

"I love you." The words tumbled out of my mouth for the first time in five years. This time, I wasn't met with cold silence.

"I dinna know what love was until I found ye, Harper. And I'll never know such love again."

We reached our peaks in a shattering unison that left us both trembling and gasping for air.

I didn't remember ever being so happy before.

Chapter 20

By the time Kamden and I drove away from the castle, with the entire staff looking on, it was nearly two hours later than originally planned. Margaret was in a tizzy about it. Which honestly—petty person that I am—gave me an immense sense of satisfaction.

"At least we won't have to wait in Margaret's barn until dark to make the walk back up here."

"Aye, 'tis the only reason I wished to tup ye the third and fourth times."

I laughed and reached for his hand as he drove us down the long pathway away from the castle. The pond stretched out to our left, and a sudden horrifying possibility entered my mind.

"Hey Kamden, did you by any chance see where Mitsy landed in the past after seeing her disappear in your dream? I mean, did she just wake up on the side of the pond or on the castle footsteps?"

"No, I dinna see anything past her vanishing before me. Why do ye ask?"

"I'm just wondering if this will work the same way as our wishes. We made them right before falling asleep, and we woke with them granted. If you throw the rock in the water, will we end up in the water, as well? We will both get sick if we end up in there tonight."

He dismissed my worry right away.

"Surely, it canna work that way. Why a person might drown being shocked in such a way. I doona think ye have anything to worry about."

I didn't feel the same optimism, but I said nothing.

It was a short drive to Margaret's home. As Kamden expected, her shed was empty and the car fit easily inside. Closing our coats, Kamden grabbed the rock, and we made the short hike back to McMillan Castle.

Lights still shone brightly through the windows of the castle as we approached it from behind, but no one seemed to be outside. With any luck, we would be able to skip the stone without anyone taking notice.

Kamden moved quickly, and I hurried to keep up with him.

"Don't throw that thing until I'm over there next to you and hanging on. I'm afraid if you throw it when we aren't touching, you'll leave me here."

He paused and extended his hand in my direction.

"Ye certainly have a lot of theories about how this wee rock will work."

"I have theories about everything. I'm a woman. I think. That's what we do."

He ignored my short-handed insult and continued to walk with me until we met the water's edge.

"Are ye ready?"

All I could think of was how cold that water must be at this time of night.

"I suppose I'll have to be."

With the eagerness of an over-excited child, Kamden pulled the rock from his pocket and skillfully sent it skipping across the water.

Everything whirled around us quickly, and the first thing I felt on the other side of consciousness was water.

Damn that Morna straight to hell.

Chapter 21

McMillan Castle—1650

S trong arms pulled me from the freezing water as I sputtered and cursed. The water was so cold, it felt like knives on my skin. From the sounds coming from Kamden, the tumble into the water was just as painful for him.

"I told you. Gah, I could've at least put on some thermals or something."

Kamden said nothing.

I should've been much more worried about the reactions of those surrounding us. What if they weren't accustomed to people landing in the pond from a different time? While Kamden believed it had happened once before, there was no reason for us to believe they were expecting us now. At least, that's what I assumed until the big, burly, dark-haired god that pulled me from the water spoke. His voice was deep, velvety, and sexy as hell.

"Lass, 'twill be easier for us to warm ye if ye stay still. I'm Baodan. We've been expecting ye for over a day now."

Baodan—I knew the name and the face now that I looked at it. His portrait hung with all the others in the great hall of McMillan Castle. This man served as laird here.

Seeing sense in his plea, I stopped flinging about and allowed the woman beside him to drape a thick, wool blanket around my shoulders. She had the most gorgeous red hair I'd ever seen.

"The first time I landed in that water, I nearly drowned. You would think Morna would come up with a better way for people to get back and forth from here. Truthfully, I think she does it for her own amusement."

It was one thing to think about the possibility that all of this could be true. It was another thing entirely to have people I'd read about in this castle's histories standing and speaking in front of me—especially when half of them were quite obviously not born of this time. Now that I was on solid ground and wrapped in something warm, I could pick them out easily—their modern vocabulary and American accents gave them away.

The woman next to me, along with three other equally stunning women, two men, and a young boy, all seemed to have traveled the same way we had at one point or another.

Kamden addressed the group despite the chatter in his teeth.

"H…how ddddd…did ye know we…we were coming?"

The little boy, who looked as excited as Kamden had before throwing the rock, raised a small pocket watch in the air and spoke.

119

"Morna told us. We're so glad you're here. It's been awhile since we've had anybody new come back."

A maternal-looking blonde stepped forward. I guessed by the way the young boy looked at her that she was his mother. "Cooper, let's get them inside and in dry clothes before we discuss anything further."

Everyone filed inside quickly, and before Kamden and I could say two words to each other, we were taken in different directions—the women off with me towards one area of the castle and Kamden off with the men in another.

It was the strangest thing to walk inside a place that had basically been my home for the better part of several years and see it through the eyes of those that owned it first. Their belongings and décor lined the halls and filled the rooms. I always felt so at home in McMillan Castle before, but I didn't feel that way at all now. It felt like all of our memories were somehow wiped away in this time. Knowing all that was yet to happen, and the castle didn't yet hold our memories broke my heart in a way I never expected.

"You don't look so good. Are you okay?"

They led me to what Kamden used as his study. In this time, the room was a small bedchamber for what appeared to be one of the castle's live-in staff.

I turned toward the second blonde. She was younger than the first and far more blunt.

"I'm fine."

I could tell she didn't quite believe me, but thankfully, she didn't press further. I didn't know how to explain to her how

120

I felt. I truly expected to find it so interesting to see the castle in this time. Instead, I just found it immensely unsettling.

The nameless woman smiled gently at me then turned to address the rest of the group.

"Why don't you guys go and check on the boys? I'll help her find something to wear, and we'll meet up with you in a bit."

No one opposed the woman's suggestion. I thought perhaps they could all see that I felt overwhelmed. Once we were alone, she faced me once again and extended her hand.

"I'm Jane. I'm a part-time resident of the castle. My husband and I split our time between here and Cagair Castle. It's a long story."

That explained why I didn't know who she was. They weren't McMillans so their portraits wouldn't have hung in the hall.

"I'm Harper. It's nice to meet you."

"There's a selection of dresses laid out for you just over there. I'll step out while you change. If you need some help, just holler. Some of it's sort of complicated."

Even as badly as I wanted out of my own wet clothes, the last thing I wanted to do was put on a garment from this time. My visceral reaction to all of this baffled me. Where had my adventurous spirit gone?

Then I thought of Kamden, and deep down I knew.

Kamden loved me, but I knew the one thing his heart always longed for the most.

Family.

121

He would love it here. He would never want to leave.
And I could never stay.

Chapter 22

Kamden never dreamed he came from such kind and conversational men. With only his grandfather as reference, he expected to be welcomed by a cold and stern group of duds. Nothing could've been more opposite of how these men were. They were kind, funny, and welcoming. Conversation flowed easily among them. Their knowledge of modern times—no doubt thanks to their modern women—made no topic too difficult to discuss.

He changed quickly. By the time he joined the men in the dining hall, they had ale and food ready and waiting for him. If he'd only known all of this was available to him as a child, he would've run away here instead of to Margaret's.

Hours passed this way. When Harper and the other women didn't join them, he assumed they were off somewhere enjoying conversation just as much as the men were. Only when all the ladies save Harper entered the dining hall did Kamden realize something was wrong.

"Where is Harper?"

Jane—he knew her name only because she moved to kiss Adwen before approaching him—walked to his side and grabbed onto his arm.

"She's gone to bed. Can I talk to you for a minute?"

Worry gripped him, and he hurried into the hallway with Jane so they could speak alone.

"Is she okay?"

"Yes, she is. Listen, I don't really know either of you. I know it's not really my place, but I just wanted to give you a heads up. Will you take some advice from someone who's been in a similar situation?"

He would take any advice he could get. If more of it had been offered to him throughout his life, perhaps he wouldn't have messed things up with Harper the first time.

"O'course I will. What's happened?"

"Harper and I had a nice long talk earlier. She didn't really open up very easily. It took some prying, and I only did so because I recognized her doe-eyed sense of dread the moment she walked into the castle. I remember feeling exactly the same way the first time I came through."

Kamden could see that Jane struggled with whether or not to say just what she wanted to. She shifted from foot to foot as she stood in front of him.

"'Tis fine, lass. My feelings are not easily hurt. Tell me what ye think I must hear."

"I'll be frank then. Honestly, I don't really know how to be anything but frank, but I was struggling to see if I could think of a way to say this more gently."

124

"Ye needn't be gentle."

Jane smiled before delivering her blow.

"Good. The two of you can't stay here."

As much as he loved it here, the thought never crossed his mind. Harper was his priority now. She would never want to live here.

"O'course. We wouldna wish to intrude on yer lives at all."

Jane laughed and shook her head.

"No, it's not that at all. We've got the room, and you wouldn't be intruding. It's Harper. She isn't meant to be in this time."

"I know that."

Jane continued to explain her rationale to him, pausing midway through when she realized what he'd said.

"I recognize myself in Harper, Kamden. I'm not meant to be in this time, either. She...what did you say? Did you say you know that?"

He nodded calmly.

"Aye. Harper would never want to stay in this time. From now on, where she goes, I go."

His new friend looked equal parts surprised and relieved.

"Oh. Well, good. That's really good. Why does she not seem sure of that, then?"

It saddened him to know that all was not yet healed in her heart.

"While Harper may have forgiven me for my folly of five years ago, that doesna mean the pain from those years has healed completely. Part of her still canna believe that I truly love her the way I do."

"Sounds to me like you need to make a grand gesture."

Kamden smiled. He had just the thing in mind.

"Aye, though I'll need some help, and if ye have access to it, a bit of magic, as well."

Chapter 23

"Good morning, love. I need ye to wake up. I've got something to show ye."

Sad and conflicted, I had fallen asleep with a heavy heart and spent all night in a tormented state that kept me tossing and turning. Despite that, I never heard Kamden come into the room. If he had any sense at all, he would've noticed that my absence from the group was a sign that something bothered me. If anything, I expected him to wake me so he could ask me about it, not to use sweet kisses down the side of my face to pull me from sleep.

Something about the soft touch of his lips against my skin prevented me from waking in the same mood I went to bed in.

I turned toward him and allowed his kiss as I spoke against his mouth.

"What is it?"

"Ye have to get up to see. I think ye'll like it."

"Is it outside?"

"No."

"Good. Give me five minutes. I'll meet you out in the hallway."

I would have to tell him today that I wouldn't be staying here. If he wished to, I wouldn't begrudge him for it, but he needed to know I wouldn't be joining him. But as I watched him leave the room, he radiated such excitement that I knew I couldn't tell him until after I enjoyed whatever it was he wanted to show me.

It took me more than five minutes to dress. Jane was right—these dresses were rather complicated, but eventually I managed.

I looked ridiculous.

"Whatever this is, it better be wor…" I stopped midsentence as I swung open the bedroom door to see Kamden down on one knee. I swallowed hard as flashbacks of that dreadful day five years ago passed through my mind.

"Harper, I see the look in yer eyes, and I beg ye not to panic. Hear me out. 'Twill not be the same."

I closed my eyes and gathered myself. I could do this if I just kept breathing and remembered all of the other things that were already so very different this time around.

"Okay. Speak."

He smiled, gathered my shaking hands in his, and kissed my knuckles before looking into my eyes.

"I love ye, Harper. I love the way yer hands show me what's in yer heart. I love the way ye love others. I love so many things about ye, but do ye know what I love most? I love that ye respected yerself enough to deny me when I dinna give ye what ye deserve. Ye taught me more that night than anyone has in my life. I'll not spend another day without ye."

He could see that I was about to interrupt him and hurried to continue so that I could not.

"This trip here has been the Christmas miracle I've waited for all my life. I've always wanted to know my family, but my home lies with ye. Marry me, Harper. Marry me and run McMillan Castle as ye always wished to. I will stand dutifully at yer side and let ye make all the decisions. Yer judgement is far better than mine. Without yer guidance in those early days, I would've given up and sold the castle to the highest bidder. Ye saved it. Ye saved me. Now let me save ye from yer own fear, for I already know what ye are thinking."

Tears streamed down my face as I listened to him. I could no longer stand and look down at him. I dropped to my knees and wrapped my arms around him.

"Oh yeah? What's that?"

"Ye are worried that I feel I'm giving something up by not staying here. Ye couldna be more wrong. Besides, I've arranged a way for us to have both. One last bit of magic to make all our Christmas wishes come true."

"What do you mean?"

"'Tis true that I doona wish to leave these people and never see them again, but I also have no wish for us to take any more swims in the middle of the night while the rest of my staff is not around.

"We canna live the past five years over again but we can change their outcome. On Christmas Eve, we will return to the

129

year we left the first time—to the snowstorm—to 2016. We have just a few days to change what happened between us last time. Let us return to 2011 tonight so we can make peace with Margaret and enjoy the days until we return to our own time together."

It wasn't only my hands that shook as I lifted myself off the ground. My knees could barely support my trembling frame as I waited for him to say the words once more.

"Ask me again."

"I love ye, Harper. I'll never love another. Will ye marry me?"

My "yes" was met with resounding applause. As he slipped the ring on my finger and gathered me into his arms, I looked down the hallway to see every resident of McMillan Castle cheering us on.

Christmas was always my favorite time of the year. I loved the snow, the songs, the family gatherings, but most of all I loved the sense of magic that hung in the air. I never dared to believe that such magic really existed and that Christmas miracles could be true until now.

After five years and two very strange time jumps, I was finally home, held tightly in Kamden's arms once again.

Chapter 24

McMillan Castle—December 24, 2016

Kamden and I married in the castle's great hall in the middle of a blizzard, on the day we returned to the present. To the castle staff and my family, it seemed like the longest engagement ever, but for us, it was just a few days. It took some work, but with the help of our new magical friend, we managed to get all of the castle's staff, the McMillans from 1650, and my grandparents to the castle so they could attend. Even Morna and her husband, Jerry, made the trip.

My grandfather officiated the ceremony. As Kamden and I sealed our vows with a kiss, I knew there would never be a Christmas as wonderful as this one. I didn't care if the storm never ended. It allowed us to bask in the love, joy, and family that surrounded us.

"Well, it seems that yer meddling has worked once again. Not only that, but ye managed to drag me out into the cold once more. Are ye pleased with yerself?"

Morna laughed and leaned into her husband as they stood with the other guests to celebrate the happy couple as they walked down the aisle as husband and wife.

"Aye, I'm verra pleased. I love Christmas."

She expected Jerry to huff in objection, but she could feel him smile against her cheek.

"I do, too."

Laughing, she turned into him and kissed him until he blushed.

"Did ye just admit to loving Christmas?"

Her husband cleared his throat and looked down at the ground.

"'Tis the season for miracles, is it not?"

She smiled and took his hand. It was time for them to return home. Her work here was done.

"Aye, and through love, all things are possible."

Turn the page for a Sneak Peek of *Love Beyond Reach* (Book 8 of Morna's Legacy Series).

Sneak Peek of Love Beyond Reach (Book 8)

Prologue

Conall Castle—Present Day

It was odd for Morna to be watched so closely in the place that had once been her childhood home. She stood nervously inside the familiar walls of her old bedchamber, twisting her head at every noise or possible footstep to make certain no other tourists or castle employees were headed their direction.

"It sure looks good, Morna. You did a really good job of making the outside look like a bunch of the other old books here. Do you have another copy? I want to read it."

A brief moment of terror filled her at the thought of Cooper opening the pages of her book and taking in the words inside. He understood far too much about everything already. The last thing he ever needed to read was every little—and sometimes scandalous—detail of her life.

"Cooper, if ye love me, ye will promise me to never, ever read what I've written. It is meant for someone else's eyes, and those are not yer own. Do ye understand?"

While young Coop usually did the exact opposite of what he was told, she could see by the concerned look in his eyes that he cared enough about her plea to listen to her this time.

"Fine, but I know what that means. It means there's the same stuff in this book as the books that Mom used to read when we lived in New York. I bet you talk about kissing Jerry in there, huh?"

She could live with it if all Cooper thought was inside those pages was a little kissing. "Aye, Cooper. I have kissed Jerry many, many times throughout our lives, and I'll admit some of those are mentioned within that wee book."

"Yuck." Cooper's expression twisted into one of disgust, and he held the book away from him as if he worried the nearness of it might cause him to absorb the words. "You don't need to say anything else. I promise to never read it. But, can I ask you one more thing? Why did you want me to come? Wouldn't E-o be able to reach that second shelf a lot better than I can?"

He surely could have, but outside of Cooper, Jerry was the only other person who knew about Morna's recent endeavor, and she wanted very much to keep it that way.

"Aye, I'm certain he would have had a much easier time of it, but Eoghanan doesna need to know anything about it. I can trust ye to keep a secret, aye? Ye know how the others feel about my meddling. I doona wish to explain it all to them."

If Cooper felt he had an important role to play in anything, he was sure to meet it head-on.

134

"Of course you can. Don't you worry. It might be a little harder, but I can climb up there and get this book placed just where you want it. How long do you think it will take for her to find it up here?"

Morna couldn't be certain. She would no longer spell anyone to do exactly as she wished them to, but she would do all she could to point the girl in the needed direction.

"I hope not verra long at all. She's here, actually. In the castle at this verra moment."

"Really?" Cooper's voice raised several octaves in his excitement. "Can you show her to me on our way out? I promise I won't say anything to her. Let's just walk by her or something, okay?"

Morna was just as keen to see the woman in person herself. "Aye, fine. Now, ye best hurry before someone finds us." She paused and pointed in the direction of the empty space where she wished the book to be placed. "Ye see there? Crawl up and slip it in place as quickly as ye can. Then, we best be on our way. Magic works best if ye set it and then release it to do as it should."

"Aye, aye, Morna. I am your humble servant, Pirate Cooper."

"A pirate? Have ye moved on from dinosaurs then?"

Cooper's voice, when he answered, sounded astonished and horrified.

"Move on from dinosaurs? Are you crazy? I don't think I could ever do that. But a man has to have varied interests. It makes him well-rounded."

135

Morna laughed at the verbatim words she'd heard from Jeffrey only a few nights before as she watched Cooper shimmy up the side of the bookcase and slip her beloved story in place.

It contained her every memory, and she hoped that when the lass found it, she would treasure every word. Only time would tell.

"I think this one is my favorite so far. There's just a feeling to it. I don't know what it is, really. Something magical about it, wouldn't you say?"

Laurel turned and awaited Marcus' response. She could tell by his glazed expression that her usually-patient friend was losing his resolve to indulge her obsession with all things old.

"You've said that about every castle. Each one is more magical than the last. Each new one is now your favorite. I'll be honest, they are all starting to look the same to me—just one big blur of stones and crumbling junk."

While many sites they'd visited over the last ten days had indeed been crumbling, Conall Castle in no way fit that description. Well-tended and magnificent, Laurel could all but see the castle's history swirling around her—could almost feel the people who lived here before.

"That's because they do keep getting more magical—I swear it—especially this one. But you know, it may just feel that way because it seems like we are the only ones here. It's lovely to have the whole castle to ourselves rather than bumping into other tourists around every corner."

Marcus laughed, and Laurel knew what he was going to say before he uttered a word. He'd complained about it for the entirety of the drive.

"It doesn't surprise me that we are the only ones here. I know lots of the places we've visited have been isolated, but this is quite literally in the middle of nowhere. If our car broke down on the way back tonight, there would be nowhere for us to stay."

Laurel found herself hoping that the car would break down just before dusk. She couldn't think of anything more enjoyable than being stranded around such beauty.

"I don't think I would care overmuch if we got stuck out here. Surely a castle as old as this wouldn't be too hard to slip into after everyone has left for the night. To sleep in a place like this would be pure heaven."

Marcus couldn't have sounded less enthused. "It probably has ghosts."

"Oh, I hope so. All of the best ones do."

"You're insane if you like ghosts." Marcus' hand on her forearm drew her attention away from the tall window she stood gazing through. "Hey, look. We're not alone, after all. Still, I agree with you that it's nice being around fewer people."

Sure enough, as Laurel turned, she could see two people approaching—an older woman accompanied by a young boy holding himself very proudly as he walked.

"Let's head down toward the other end, Marcus, so they have this area of the castle to themselves."

The woman and boy said nothing to them as they passed, but Laurel found herself struck by the intensity of the unabashed stare she received from them both. She gave them a friendly smile in return, and the young boy raised his left hand and waved in greeting before they went on their way.

"Did you see the way they both stared at me? Has my blouse popped open or something?"

Laurel looked self-consciously down at herself as she tried to make sense of their wide, questioning eyes.

"No. Everything is covered as far as I can tell. Maybe they recognized you."

Laurel laughed and continued to move down the long hallway toward the last room at the end.

"Did you see how small that child was? There is no way he knows who I am. If his parents let him read one of my books at his age, then God help him. No, it definitely wasn't that. Maybe they were staring at you, and I just mistook the direction of the boy's gaze."

"Because I'm black? Come on, Laurel. Surely you think better of them than that."

Laurel couldn't tell if he was joking, but it wouldn't surprise her if he wasn't. Marcus had so many wonderful qualities. While his humility was to be admired, it drove her crazy just how incapable he was of recognizing his own attractiveness.

"No, Marcus. I most definitely didn't think they were staring at you because you are black. Perhaps they were staring at you because the only other human I've seen with your shape is

138

the guy who plays Captain America, and he's just a freak of nature."

Marcus huffed and stepped out of her sight and into the room to their right.

"I didn't even make eye contact with them. They were definitely staring at you. Let's just forget it. I can already predict what you are going to say about this room."

Laurel remained just outside the doorway as she awaited his prediction.

"Oh yeah? What's that?"

"You are going to say that out of all the castles and all the rooms you've seen, this is by far your favorite."

She knew he teased her, but regardless, he was bound to be wrong. The room that lay ahead of her couldn't possibly beat the tower room they saw in the castle two days before.

"Let's just see about that, shall we?"

Determined to come up with a reaction completely opposite of what Marcus expected, Laurel stepped inside, looked around, and found herself completely unable to do so.

The room was perfect in every way. The things she loved most in all the world lined three out of the four walls—books.

"It drives me crazy when you are right. This beats the tower."

"I knew you were going to say that. I knew it even before I stepped inside. I read about it in the guidebook and knew you'd love it. I can see by the happy, glazed expression on your face that you'll be in here a while. I think I'll go explore the dungeon while you do so. I'll come back for you in a bit."

Marcus nudged her playfully before leaving her alone in the room. Once he was gone, she inhaled deeply and smiled. The smell of books gave her the same kind of energy coffee did for some. She thrived off of them, lived in them, made her own living from them. In a room full of books, she felt at home.

She knew that the books lining the shelves didn't quite fit with the historical nature of the castle. The bindings and covers were enough to tell her that none of them could be more than a hundred years old. Still, that knowledge did nothing to damper her love for what surrounded her now.

She moved to the far wall and slowly trailed her fingers along the spines, moving row after row, bottom to top. It was a game she often played in libraries—whatever number popped in her mind first was the number of books she would count before she pulled the next one she would read. The top row required her to stand on the tips of her toes, but she was still three books away from landing on her number, so tradition required her to reach.

It took little for her to pull it from its place. As she latched fully onto it for the first time, she glanced over her shoulder to see a soft, empty chair in the corner of the room.

Marcus would occupy himself for ages exploring the castle grounds. It wouldn't hurt anyone a bit for her to take a moment to peruse the books on the shelves in this room. If the spines of most of the books were any indication, most of them weren't written in English, but she hoped that once inside she would find enough recognizable words to tell her what classic she'd pulled from the shelves. It was bound to be something everyone knew—no doubt a *Jane Eyre* or a *Treasure Island.*

The chair was old, and for a moment, she feared it would collapse underneath her. But as she settled in more fully, it seemed to wrap her up in a way that invited her to do nothing more than read.

She opened the book gently. While it surprised her to see that the words were English, it was the handwritten note inside that piqued her interest in a way nothing else ever had.

"To whomever finds this book, you should know that it was meant just for you. Tuck it away in your bag, hide it beneath your shirt, but whatever you do, do not return it to the place from which it rested before. For many would read the pages contained within and dismiss my every memory, my every word, as nothing more than fiction. But you, my first and last reader, will read these words and hear the truth in them.

"Read these words. Love them, tend to them, believe them, and then once you've made peace with the truth, come and find me. By my story's end, you will know just where."

Until we may meet,

Morna Conall

"Damn," Laurel whispered the word aloud to herself, shaking her head at the book with mesmerized awe. Whatever the reason for such strange words, the author must have known that it would be impossible for the reader who stumbled upon them to do anything other than read on. She didn't know anyone whose curiosity would allow them to do differently.

Smiling at the wit and the wonder of it, Laurel happily flipped to the next page and continued, never suspecting for a moment how such an act would change her life forever.

Read all the books in Morna's Legacy Series:

LOVE BEYOND TIME (BOOK 1)

LOVE BEYOND REASON (BOOK 2)

A CONALL CHRISTMAS – A NOVELLA (BOOK 2.5)

LOVE BEYOND HOPE (BOOK 3)

LOVE BEYOND MEASURE (BOOK 4)

IN DUE TIME – A NOVELLA (BOOK 4.5)

LOVE BEYOND COMPARE (BOOK 5)

LOVE BEYOND DREAMS (BOOK 6)

LOVE BEYOND BELIEF (BOOK 7)

A MCMILLAN CHRISTMAS – A NOVELLA (BOOK 7.5)

About The Author

Bethany Claire is the USA Today Bestselling Author of the Scottish time travel romance novels in Morna's Legacy Series.

Bethany's love of storytelling has been a lifelong passion but, convinced it would serve her best to follow a "conventional" career path, she tucked that passion away and went off to college.

Fast forward four years and about six major changes later, she realized the stories simply were not going to stay tucked away. Months away from graduating with a degree in elementary education, she finally realized writing was the only career that would make her happy.

So one day in the middle of a summer education course, she got up in the middle of class and walked to the registrar's office and withdrew from the university on the spot. Since then, she has devoted herself to writing full time and is following her dreams.

Read more about Bethany at www.bethanyclaire.com.

Connect With Me Online

http://www.bethanyclaire.com
http://twitter.com/BClaireAuthor
http://facebook.com/bethanyclaire
http://www.pinterest.com/bclaireauthor

If you enjoyed reading *A McMillan Christmas,* I would appreciate it if you would help others enjoy this book, too:

Recommend it. Help other readers find this book by recommending it to friends, readers' groups and discussion boards.

Review it. Please tell other readers why you like this book by reviewing it at the retailer of your choice. If you do write a review, please send me an email to bclaire@bethanyclaire.com so I can thank you with a personal email, or you can visit my website at http://www.bethanyclaire.com

Join the Bethany Claire Newsletter!

Sign up for my newsletter to receive up-to-date information of books, new releases, events, and promotions.

http://bethanyclaire.com/contact.php#mailing-list

Acknowledgments

There is so much work that goes into each book besides the writing. For the endless patience and keen eyes of my team members, I am eternally grateful. To Mom: There is nobody that has a better assistant than I do. Thank you for hanging on with me this past year while I took the time I needed to rest and recoup. Your belief that things would get better and the words would return allowed me to believe that they would, too. Slowly, I've fallen in love with writing again.

To my proofreaders: Elizabeth, Karen, Johnetta, & Melissa—a special thank you to you guys for always being so quick with the turnaround and for your helpful suggestions. To Marsha, Diane, Lora, Kris, Evie, Jennifer, & Deanna, thanks for agreeing to help me out on this one. The extra eyes are always a help.

To Dj: Thanks for always being so agreeable and squeezing me in. You're a lifesaver.

41338961R00092

Made in the USA
Middletown, DE
10 March 2017